A PROMISE
AND A RAINBOW

A PROMISE AND A RAINBOW

The Double Dutch Club Series #3

MABEL ELIZABETH SINGLETARY

MOODY PUBLISHERS

CHICAGO

© 2008 by
MABEL ELIZABETH SINGLETARY

Cover Design: Trevell Southhall, TS Design
                www.tsdesignstudio.net (http://www.tsdesignstudio.net)
Cover Image: Punchstock
Inside Design: Ragont Design
Editor: Kathryn Hall

Library of Congress Cataloging-in-Publication Data

Singletary, Mabel Elizabeth.
    A promise and a rainbow / by Mabel Elizabeth Singletary.
      p. cm. — (Double Dutch Club series; #3)
    Summary: While the Double Dutch Club shares fun and competition, Rachel is in Chicago with her cousin Ronnie, with whom she shares instant dislike, trying to find a way to get through what promises to be a very difficult summer.
    ISBN-13: 978-0-8024-2255-2
    ISBN-10: 0-8024-2255-1
    [1. Cousins—Fiction. 2. Interpersonal relations—Fiction. 3. Rope skipping—Fiction. 4. Competition (Psychology)—Fiction. 5. Friendship—Fiction. 6. Christian life—Fiction. 7. African Americans—Fiction. 8. Chicago (Ill.)—Fiction.] I. Title.

PZ7.S61767Pro 2008
[Fic]—dc22

2008004598

1 3 5 7 9 10 8 6 4 2

Printed in the United States of America

*This book is dedicated to
those who allow themselves to see past rainstorms,
believing God's rainbows will follow.*

Contents

Chapter One

Big Plans

Rachel Carter ran across the playground, waving a sheet of paper in her hand high above her head. Screaming the entire way, "I did it! I did it!" she headed directly to the blacktop where she knew she'd find the other members of the Double Dutch Club. Carla's feet had just begun rocking back and forth, giving every indication she was only seconds away from leaping into the ropes. Suddenly everything came to a screeching halt. "Look what you did, Rachel," Tanya scolded. "I wanted to see Carla top the jump I just did, and you messed it all up."

Rachel could see Tanya was pretty mad, but even getting yelled at by her couldn't do anything to spoil her great mood. And surely, Rachel wasn't going to let a few short words diminish in any way the terrific news she carried in her hand. Though breathing hard, she tried to explain. "I didn't mean to . . . I just wanted to . . ." Tanya waved her hand in disgust. "Save it, Rachel. Don't matter now no way."

Nancy could see the hurt on Rachel's face and attempted to defend her abrupt but obviously innocent interruption. "She must have something very good to tell us, or I don't think she would have rushed over here and got in the way of Carla's jump like that."

"We don't have much time left," Brittany warned. "That bell's gonna sound off real soon, and we'll be on our way back inside. I think you coulda waited a coupla minutes more, Rachel. Nothing coulda been that important."

Tanya gave some thought to what Nancy had said and walked over a little closer to where Rachel was standing. Her tone was serious, but Rachel was glad because she suspected that maybe Tanya was interested in hearing her news. Tanya stuck one leg out in front of the other and folded her arms. "So, what's so important?"

And as usual, if Tanya wanted to know something, so did Carla. "Yeah," she echoed. "What's *soooo* important?"

Rachel, still panting from running, almost couldn't get her words out. "Mr. . . . Mr. . . . Whitman's test . . . I passed it!"

All of the girls, including Lindsey, who up to this point hadn't expressed any interest, also circled around Rachel. And everyone was surprised that Lindsey was the one who took Rachel to task for messing up their jump. "It's good you passed, but you coulda waited a few more seconds just like Brittany said. It was almost my turn, and you got in the way and messed us all up. Thanks, Rachel."

Rachel didn't understand why the other girls weren't excited about her great news.

"You don't get it," she insisted. "*Now* I don't have to go to summer school. I can jump with the club! Don't you think that's the best possible news you've ever heard in your whole life?"

Carla, once again imitating Tanya, now stood with her arms folded too. She stared at Rachel as though expecting more. After all, only the most earth-shattering, extraordinary, absolutely phenomenal news could be important enough to stop the group right in the middle of a jump. And by no means did Carla think the news Rachel brought was worthy enough to fit into any of those categories.

Tanya picked up the ropes and started tying them up. "It's good ya passed, but it really ain't no big deal. Ya know he gives the same test at the end of every school year. All you had to do was ask somebody who had him last year, and they woulda helped you out."

Rachel was starting to get annoyed that her friends weren't as happy as she thought they should have been about her passing the final test of what was her most difficult subject all school year. She clenched her fists tightly. "I don't care that he gives the same test! The important thing here is that I, Rachel Carter, passed Mr. Whitman's final math test for the year with flying colors! And I did it because I studied, not because somebody told me what was gonna be on the test ahead of time."

Nancy's eyes widened like saucers. "You mean you got an 'A'? I have heard it is almost impossible to get an 'A' from Mr. Whitman." Smiling pleasantly, she waited for Rachel to answer.

"An 'A'? Who said anything about an 'A'? Nobody gets an 'A' from Mr. Whitman. He makes the test way too hard for anybody to get an 'A.'"

Brittany stepped up to Rachel and got very close to her face. Looking directly into her eyes, it was as though she believed her staring would somehow give her the power to separate fact from fiction. She decided to question her further. "So, the reason you're so excited is because you got a 'B'?"

It was clear Rachel was becoming annoyed with her friends. "A 'B'? How many kids do you know who took that math class with 'Wither 'em down Whitman' passed his final and lived to tell about it?"

Just then, Nancy started to laugh and likewise so did Tanya, Lindsey, Carla, and Brittany. Rachel realized the girls had been putting her on. They were very glad she had passed her test. "We are very happy you passed," Nancy said, putting up her hand to give Rachel a high five. As soon as Rachel tapped Nancy's hand, she moved on to each of the girls and received a high five from them all. "Good job!" Tanya said. "I had Mr. Whitman too, and I just barely made it through."

"Well, if you have any more trouble, I'll help you out!" Rachel joked. That good feeling she had when she first came running across the playground had just come back.

Tanya had already thought of some new routines for the club and couldn't wait to share them and show them to Coach Hughes. Everyone's mind was on one thing and one thing only. They were looking forward to two whole months of nothing but Double Dutch, Double Dutch, and more Double Dutch. Soon Rachel found herself laughing as loudly as her teammates. She had passed her math exam, and absolutely nothing was standing in the way of having the best summer ever. "I know there's only a little time left, but if you want, I'll turn."

Rachel's offer satisfied everyone. And in the few minutes remaining, she took one end of the ropes, while Lindsey took the other end, and turned. Nancy,

Carla, Brittany, and Tanya grinned and giggled while alternately jumping in and out of them.

On the other side of the playground, Amber's teacher had taken her class outside for a short recess. And just as Amber was known to do, as soon as her teacher's attention was drawn in another direction, she secretly made her way over to the blacktop to meet up with her seventh-grade friends.

She successfully reached the area where the girls were jumping, but was careful to keep hidden behind the old great oak. "Pssst," she said, keeping her voice low while at the same time trying to get everyone's attention. She prayed her teacher wouldn't notice her absence. She hoped Mrs. Bellamy hadn't formed a search party and begun asking the other students if they knew where Amber had gone. Nonetheless, she decided to take her chances and made an attempt to quickly get in on the fun. "Let me get in a jump?" she asked, revealing herself when she stepped from behind the tree.

"Hold it!" Tanya said, putting up her hand like Mrs. Kelly, the crossing guard.

"First of all, you're not supposed to be over here. And second of all, you're not supposed to be over here."

Amber decided to make use of her angelic baby face. It always came in handy when she wanted the older girls to let her have her way about something. "Aw, please let me jump," she pleaded.

Tanya had a real hard time saying no to Amber. She liked the way Amber looked up to her and the other girls in the club; she often felt like Amber was the baby sister she wished she had. So if allowing her to get in a jump sometimes spoiled her, Tanya was more than ready to take the blame. "Okay, but you'd better make it quick. Recess is just about over. And if you get caught, ain't nothing we can do."

"Thanks, Tanya," she said as she took a big breath and leaped inside the ropes.

"Look at me!" Amber yelled to the others while she jumped and turned and lifted her hands high in the air.

"Okay," Lindsey told her. "I think you've jumped long enough."

Amber protested. "No, I haven't, and you can't tell me when to come out."

"You're right," Lindsey said, pointing toward the far end of the field. "I can't, but your teacher, Mrs. Bellamy, sure can!"

Amber stopped jumping and stood facing Mrs. Bellamy. With her hands on her hips, she looked very small from the spot where she was waiting for her long-lost student to return. Amber couldn't clearly see her face, but it didn't take much to imagine how dissatisfied Mrs. Bellamy was as she waited on the other side of the field. She secretly wished her teacher could stay as small as she appeared from the distance where she'd seen her when she stopped jumping. At least she wished it could be so for the rest of the day, or until everything was back to normal. Then she wouldn't have to worry about the punishment that she was certain awaited her.

Amber waved good-bye to the other girls, shook her head, and walked straight toward Mrs. Bellamy as though taking full responsibility for the really tough spot she had managed to get herself into.

"Right now, I don't think I'd wanna be Amber," Lindsey said as she picked up the ropes to begin turning again.

"Yeah," Carla agreed. "We probably won't see her sneaking around during recess again no time soon."

Nancy was braced to jump into the ropes when the bell sounded. "That means I will get to jump first tomorrow!"

Lindsey began wrapping up the ropes, and Nancy helped her. "So what days are we gonna get together and jump?" Rachel asked.

Tanya, who had begun walking toward the building, suddenly stopped. "What days?"

Everyone could hear the anxiousness in Rachel's voice. "We only got two weeks left, and then it'll be summer vacation! We won't have to worry about recess or lunchtime then. We'll be able to jump Double Dutch any time we want!"

Carla started helping Lindsey and Nancy with the ropes. "I might be getting a babysitting job this summer, working for Mrs. Washington over on Crenshaw Avenue. So I can't say if I'll be able to jump all the time, but I'll at least try to come some days."

"What about you, Tanya?" Rachel asked. "You'll be able to jump, won't you?"

Rachel was pretty sure if Tanya couldn't make it, chances were slim to none that the others wouldn't feel like they had to come either.

"I should be able to make it long as my grandma doesn't need me to do anything for her."

Hearing Tanya say she'd come was like music to Rachel's ears. Feeling a lot more confident, she then pointed at Nancy and Lindsey. They could hear the strength in her voice. "And you two?"

"I don't know," Nancy was quick to say. "But I will try very hard to be here."

"I'm supposed to watch my little brother," Lindsey said. "But I guess I can bring him along. He won't get in the way."

Brittany wore a tremendous smile as she stepped up to the others. "I'm going to take dance lessons this summer, and I can't wait!"

Rachel immediately decided she wasn't going to let Brittany get off so easily. "Well, nobody dances all day.

There's gotta be some time in there to jump with us, right?"

"Yeah, there'll be time for jumping too," Brittany assured her.

As the girls walked together toward the building, each one had her own beautiful vision of the summer ahead. Rachel focused her thoughts on her own special plans. And they were big plans for a summer filled with days of spending time with her friends, talking, laughing, and most of all doing the one thing they all loved so much. They would have plenty of time to jump Double Dutch. And as Rachel smiled inwardly, she asked herself, *What could be better than that?*

Chapter Two

First
a Promise . . .

TWO days later, Rachel found herself riding in the car with her dad and daydreaming about the wonderful summer she was creating and planning in her mind.

She was feeling great inside and freely entertained the thought that soon she'd have two months of carefree days. She imagined herself getting up early and heading over to Grover Cleveland Elementary School where the next part of her plan called for meeting up with the girls of the Double Dutch Club. Once together, they would have all the time in the world to make up lots of new routines and jump each one of them to perfection. This way, by the time the next competition came around, Rachel knew they'd be more ready than ever.

Without any warning, she suddenly spoke out loud. That's when her father became privy to her plans. "Yep," she said confidently and wearing an expression to match. That's what we've got to do. We've got to work harder now, 'cause we've got a title to defend."

Rachel thought about how hard they'd practiced when getting ready for the "North Carolina Jump Off" and how all that practicing had really paid off. She quickly relived the moment she and her teammates accepted their trophies as the first place winners in the competition.

While studying the darkening sky quickly forming above them, Mr. Carter took a moment to give his daughter some encouragement. "I guess who ever those other teams are, they'd better look out, because it sounds like the Double Dutch Club is real serious."

"That's for sure," Rachel said fearlessly, "because when we jump, our team means business!"

Within seconds, the storm that Mr. Carter had sensed was brewing suddenly burst forth in the form of a torrential downpour. He attempted to adjust the windshield wipers and set them to move at full speed. But no matter how fast they moved, it did very little to help. Seeing the road ahead was more than difficult; it was impossible. As he turned the steering wheel carefully, he shared with his daughter what he knew he had to do. "I think we'd better pull over," he said. "This rain's coming down way too hard."

Rachel instinctively nodded her head yes. She had been busy thinking about her plans for summer vacation. So it wasn't until the very minute when her father told her that he was going to park the car that she realized how hard the rain was coming down. But it was the unexpected sound of loud, crashing thunder sneaking up on them that kidnapped her attention and forced her to take notice of what was happening. She quickly agreed that her father was right. They needed to stop.

"Right here looks good," her dad said, maneuvering the car to the far right side of the road. He parked just about two hundred feet from a small bridge located on the outskirts of town. "Soon as it tapers off, we'll be on our way."

Rachel smiled and was clearly in favor of the plan. She enjoyed the sound of the rain beating on the roof of the car. It reminded her of the way it sometimes sounded at night when she lay in bed listening to the drops beat rhythmically on the roof above her bedroom. It was a forceful sound, but at the same time a peaceful one. And sometimes she'd close her eyes and see herself jumping Double Dutch to the patterns she could hear created by the falling rain. Temporarily surrendering her thoughts about jumping, Rachel strained to see what was going on outside. But it was harder to see out of the front and side windows now than it had been just a few moments ago. Her dad could tell by the slight tremor in her voice that she was starting to feel afraid. "Think it's gonna stop soon?" she asked him.

"I hope so," he said, tapping out a little beat on the steering wheel. He knew this always made Rachel smile. And it did. "If we don't get home soon, your mom will start to worry, and we don't want that."

"No," Rachel agreed, "we don't want that."

The two of them sat in the car for close to thirty minutes, waiting for the rainstorm to run its course. Mr. Carter helped the time to pass quickly by telling Rachel a funny story. He was sure it would keep her mind off the storm and hopefully drive her fears far away.

He had just finished his second story when the rain came to an end. The sun began revealing itself a little bit at a time. Soon it was positioned high in the sky like the crowned victor who had successfully overtaken and smothered the darkness that had been caused by the storm. All of a sudden, Rachel saw something special. Ignoring the pellets of rain settling outside her window, she rolled it down to get a better look. "Look, Dad! Over there!" she exclaimed while pointing to a magnificent scene way beyond the bridge. "I didn't know they were real!"

Her dad rolled down his window and stuck his head partially outside of it. It seemed like a minute had passed before he said anything at all. And when he did speak, it was plain to see that the wonderful sight had captured his attention too. "Beautiful, isn't it?"

Rachel sat studying the scene before her. She reached her hand out in front of her face and outlined what she saw by tracing it with her finger. "I don't think I ever saw anything so pretty."

"Rainbows are a gift," her father told her, ". . . a gift from God."

"From God? . . . how's that?" Rachel asked.

"Well, I think they are," he added.

"Why do you think that?" She wanted to know more.

"I don't know. Maybe 'cause they just seem to show up at the right time. Sometimes when things look like they might stay dark forever, all of a sudden you look up and you see one. It's like a sign of hope telling us we can believe that things will be all right."

"You mean, like the storm?" she said.

"Yeah, like the storm. It was so bad I had to pull over for a while, but all the time I knew it would end soon. All we had to do was wait it out. And as you can see, it's okay now and safe for us to move on. It doesn't mean there won't be other storms at some other time. But at least for now, that one is long gone."

"Don't you think it woulda been better to see the rainbow first?"

Mr. Carter paused a moment to think before he answered Rachel's question.

"No," he said, smiling at his daughter.

"Well, I do. Maybe I wouldn't have been so afraid if I knew the rainbow was coming."

"But sometimes," he said softly, "we have to wait a little while to be able to see the good things God may have for us."

"I don't know what you mean."

"If you saw rainbows every day, would you think they were as special as the one we're looking at right now?"

Rachel gazed out at the rainbow again, and her dad could see that she was starting to understand. "No, I guess it wouldn't be so special then." She pointed at the beautiful hue of colors that comprised it. Together they acted as a backdrop that had willingly spread itself across the late afternoon sky.

"I know it's pretty, but what makes it special?"

"Your faith makes it special," he explained.

Rachel's eyes questioned her father's words. "My faith?"

"Your faith will cause you to search and to wait for the next one. We can see that one," he said as he pointed toward the sky. "But you'll have to trust and believe for the next one."

"You mean, like expecting it?"

"Yes, like expecting it."

"Do you expect them, Daddy?"

When Mr. Carter smiled, he did so with such confidence that it made Rachel feel good just to be on the receiving end of it. "I just happen to be a person who believes that rainbows are the reminders we need every now and again. They let us know God hasn't forgotten His promise to us. So to answer your question, yes, I expect them."

Rachel heard the word *promise* and became even more interested in what her father had to say. "What kind of promise? I hope you don't mean like the time Tanya told us if we let her jump first for five straight days, she'd pay for the whole team to go to the movies. Then after we let her jump, she said she was just kidding."

"No . . . not exactly. All of God's promises are true. Like believing He's always here with us."

"You mean, like when it was raining real hard and I got scared?"

"I mean . . . all the time. Whether it's raining or even if it's the most beautiful sunny day you've ever seen . . . God's right there in the middle of it with us. First there's a promise. Then just when it looks like it may not come true, God goes and paints us a beautiful rainbow across the sky where anybody and everybody can see. It's our reminder that His promises are true and we can believe them forever."

Rachel was pleased with her father's explanation. "Thank you, Daddy."

"Thanks? . . . for what?"

"I'm just glad you told me that there's a promise in front of every rainbow. I'm gonna remember that. 'Cause the next time I see one, I'll know another promise has been kept that somebody somewhere was waitin' for."

This time it was Mr. Carter who looked pleased. "Now I'm glad."

Mr. Carter started the car and began to drive off. Rachel continued to stare out of her window, studying the first real rainbow she had ever seen. She wanted her memory to act like a camera and record the picture so that she would always remember. As her father drove away, she mouthed each and every color embodied in what she considered an exquisite sight. Rachel knew she would now always look for a rainbow after a storm.

Even though she knew there was no guarantee one would be where she could see it, she knew it was a possibility.

Rachel Carter made up her mind that afternoon— not only would she look for a rainbow after the next storm—she was going to expect it. And she could hardly wait to see another one. Somehow getting stuck in what seemed like a horrible rainstorm had turned out to be a good thing. She had learned something new and enjoyed listening to her dad tell about God's special promise. Rachel knew this was an afternoon drive with her father she'd remember forever.

So as her father drove across the bridge and headed toward home, she stared at the rainbow until she could no longer see it in the sky. She whispered to herself a gentle reminder, "First a promise, then a rainbow."

Chapter Three

Next to
the Last Day

The days leading up to summer had flown by even faster than Rachel could have hoped. Something on the inside must have been preparing her for a relaxing summer two days before school ended. On this particular morning, she found herself rushing out the door desperately attempting to catch her school bus. She could still see the bus in the distance and figured she must have missed it by only seconds. But in this case, seconds and minutes meant the same thing. She hadn't reached her bus stop in time. So now she was faced with the burden of going back home and pleading with her mom, who was rushing off to work, for a ride to school.

Rachel figured her mother must have also started feeling the "easing in" of summer. Mrs. Carter didn't give her daughter the lecture on the importance of punctuality that Rachel knew she deserved. Certainly she would have gotten it right away if the same thing had happened in September. "Thanks, Mom!" she said, grabbing hold of her books and rushing to get out of the car."

"Have a good day," her mother said as she watched Rachel enter the building.

The excitement that filled the halls and classrooms at Grover Cleveland Elementary School that morning was like a welcoming fresh breeze of air that touched every person who walked in its path. All the conversations, footsteps, and laughter meshed together like a wonderful symphony playing out its last movement with vigor—all the while anticipating the waiting applause. It was next to the last day before summer vacation and the atmosphere was all abuzz with news of vacations and special activities planned for faculty and students alike. Even the ladies in the cafeteria smiled their biggest smiles on this day. Mouths dropped when they willingly let Tony Sinclair, known for his ability to be difficult, have two cookies just because he asked for them.

Finding an unhappy face was next to impossible on this day, and Rachel Carter's was no exception as she hurried herself into homeroom to turn in her books. She had hoped to meet up with Tanya, Brittany, Carla, Lindsey, Nancy, and Amber before the bell, but was well aware that wasn't going to happen because she had shown up so late.

The problem started when she had trouble locating Mr. Whitman's math book and was determined not to pay a fine for its disappearance. Trying to track it down had been the real reason she had missed her bus. But after digging through her closet for the third time, she finally hit pay dirt and emerged with the elusive text in her hand. The way she proudly carried the book into class, one would have thought she was toting a rare and priceless literary work penned by a well-known but long-deceased famous author.

For Rachel, handing in that book was the last tie soon to be broken between herself and Mr. Whitman. She had passed his class and didn't want to tax her brain cells one second longer than she had to. At least she didn't plan to use them for the next ten weeks, if she could get away with it.

In her overanxious desire to get rid of the text, Rachel burst into homeroom, lifting up her book and declaring, "Here it is!" She didn't even stop at her seat to let Mr. Whitman finish taking attendance. Her urgency made one think she believed she might lose the book again just by sitting down in her assigned seat. In a move that seemed like a combination of boldness, bravery, and just end-of-the-school-year foolishness, she plopped the book on his desk.

When she turned around and found herself greeted by absolute silence, she knew she had just made a gigantic mistake. Quietly, she reached out her hands and picked up the math book, removing it from her teacher's desk. Hugging it close to her, she stepped silently to her desk and sat down. Without uttering a word, she put her head down on the book. Rachel was careful not to make eye contact with the one person who held the power to give her what she saw as "earned relief" from a math book she thought was way too heavy to carry for even one more minute.

"Thank you, Miss Carter," Mr. Whitman uttered while checking off her name on the attendance sheet. "One might get the impression you were anxious to begin your summer vacation. But I must remind you, there is still one whole day left."

Rachel could tell from Mr. Whitman's tone of voice he meant business and that an apology was expected. "I'm sorry, Mr. Whitman," she offered in the most apologetic voice she could muster. He nodded his head to let her know he had accepted her words of remorse. "And please see that it doesn't happen again," he added.

Although his face was partially hidden by his attendance roster, when Rachel looked up, she could see that he had the biggest smile on his face she'd ever seen. In fact, when she thought about it, she hadn't seen him smile very much the entire school year. *Maybe,* she thought, *teachers get excited about the end of the school year and the beginning of summer just like we do.* She didn't dare ask, but deep down she knew she was right. Mr. Whitman was happy too that the school year was just about over.

After he had collected all of the books, he let the class play a math relay game, and Rachel's team won by three points. She enjoyed the game and realized maybe math was a pretty good subject after all.

Since it was next to the last day of school, the students were able to have lunch outside. This special event was called the "Grover Cleveland Schoolwide Picnic." Students brought their blankets and shared lunches with their friends. There were lots of games and fun activities held, like relay races. And there was even a horseshoe contest. Teachers, students from all grades, as well as parent-helpers, all played and competed in many of the games and events.

The girls from the Double Dutch Club roared with laughter when they saw their sixth-grade teacher, Mrs. Richards, working hard to keep a ping-pong ball balanced on the end of a teaspoon. Even Mr. Redshaw donned white sneakers and a New York Mets baseball cap as he took on the role of pitcher in the staff versus students' softball game. And many parents had joined in and helped out by baking cookies, cakes, and pies to make the day even more special.

It was amusing to watch Mr. Redshaw winding up his arm and preparing for what could be his third strike on one of the sixth graders. He carefully focused on the spot directly above home plate where he would have to throw the ball in order to get the call his team needed. Suddenly, and without any warning, the ball was put in motion and went hurling toward home plate. Mrs. Lattimer, the girls physical education teacher, threw back her arm and with her thumb pointing behind her, yelled at the top of her lungs: "STRIKE THREE, YOU'RE OUT!"

Everyone on Mr. Redshaw's team jumped for joy. And Mr. Redshaw felt great knowing he only had one more person to strike out in order to end the game with a five-to-two victory. Students and teachers alike waited in suspense to see who the batter was going to be. Mr. Redshaw's face showed nothing but confidence, which stretched from one side of his face completely to the other, when he realized the next batter was Theodore Lane, also known as "The Professor." After all, he thought, the only thing anyone ever saw "The Professor" doing was reading.

Mr. Redshaw almost considered giving him a break because he knew this would be the easiest out of the game. Once again, the field was quiet. The silence may have been even more intense than the final pitch of a World Series game. Theodore stood at the plate with his bat in hand and his concentration on the oncoming pitch. Mr. Redshaw threw the ball. And on that first pitch, the sound of the cracking bat against it sent the ball sailing far beyond the reach of Mr. Conner, who was covering the outfield.

"The Professor's" hit spelled only one thing—home run. And with three people on base, it equaled four runs in all. By the time "The Professor" stepped across home plate, the score had become six to five. This very capable young man had proven another of his abilities to the onlookers at the Grover Cleveland field day. In addition to being a genius, he could play softball too.

In spite of the surprising upset, everyone enjoyed the excitement of the game. When it was over, Mr. Redshaw and his team shook hands with "The Professor" and all of the students on his team. They even voted him "most valuable player" for the day. From the look on Theodore's face, you would have thought he had just been awarded a Nobel Prize.

At the end of the day, students and teachers were equally tired, but it was a given that each and every one would be in attendance bright and early the next day.

After all, it was going to be the last day of school. And when it was over, everyone would be ready to welcome the onset of a brand-new summer recess.

Chapter Four

Surprise . . . !

WHEN Rachel got home, she couldn't wait to tell her parents about her special day at school. She smiled to herself and thought, *If every school day could be like this one, there would be no need for summer vacation at all.*

Even Coach Hughes must have been feeling the excitement surrounding the end of the school year because she ended their last practice of the term earlier than usual. Then she wished all the girls a wonderful summer. That may have been their last formal practice, but Rachel and the team had planned to spend the entire summer jumping for fun. And Rachel Carter was someone who couldn't wait to get started.

All the way home, she wouldn't allow herself to think about anything else.

Putting her key in the door, she opened it and tossed her book bag full of returned work, used notebooks, and other school supplies as far up the stairs as she could. But she knew all the while she'd better make sure her belongings were in her room by the time her parents came home. Then Rachel went straight to the kitchen and began searching for just the right snack. She settled on a bright red apple sitting in the fruit basket placed in the middle of the table. Carefully she turned it around, making sure to find what she thought would be the juiciest place to start.

Just as she was about to take her very first bite, a note that had been folded and placed against the bottom of the basket caught her attention. It had the name RACHEL printed in large letters on the outside. She reached for it and quickly lifted the top of the note to read the message. It simply read, *See you at dinner. Love, Mom and Dad.*

Right away, all kinds of thoughts raced through Rachel's mind. What was going on? Had something special been planned? Maybe they wanted to celebrate their daughter's passing Mr. Whitman's math course. Anyone who ever had a class with Mr. Whitman knew that, by the end of the year, if you passed his exam, you deserved a reward.

But whatever was going on, Rachel was anxious for them to come home. So she decided to keep herself busy until they got there. She wanted to make sure everything downstairs looked nice. She took out the special floral dinner plates and the good silverware, the way her mom did whenever company came. She carefully set the table and even dusted the furniture.

Perhaps her parents would have Rachel close her eyes and walk her out to the garage. And when she opened them, there before her would be the beautiful twelve-speed racing bike she'd been admiring in the window of the cycling shop downtown. She visualized herself riding against the wind and making it on time every day to her favorite destination—the blacktop.

Whatever the surprise might be, Rachel wanted to be ready. She charged up the stairs and cleared away her things in the hallway. She took a moment to stand in front of her mirror and practiced to perfection her best look of surprise. She decided that putting in some time straightening up her room wouldn't hurt either. But all of her efforts stopped when she heard the sound of a key unlocking the front door. She knew it was her dad because she could hear him whistling. Mr. Carter usually whistled when something good had happened or was about to happen. So when Rachel heard him whistling his favorite tune, she knew it was a good sign.

Hurrying down the stairs to meet him, she greeted

her father with a hug and a great big grin. "Hi, Dad," she announced as she peeked to see if he held anything special behind his back.

"Somebody's in a real good mood today," he said. "Could it have anything to do with the fact that tomorrow is the last day of school?"

"Maybe, but that's not the only reason." Rachel studied her dad as though waiting to see if he was going to give away any information about the surprise. "I got the note."

"The note?" he asked.

"Yeah, Dad, the note." Rachel pointed toward the kitchen. "The one you and Mom left on the table."

"Oh, that note." Mr. Carter replied. "As soon as your mother gets home, we'll talk about it."

"Can't you just tell me now?" Rachel pleaded. ". . . please, Dad?"

"It's really your mom's news, so I think we should wait for her, don't you?"

Hearing that, Rachel knew it was no use. She wasn't going to find out anything about her surprise until her mother got home. "Okay," she conceded. She glanced up at the clock on the kitchen wall and felt somewhat relieved knowing that in another forty-five minutes or so the big mystery would be solved once and for all. And as though sitting there in the kitchen watching that clock would make time move faster, Rachel stayed in her seat and kept a close eye on the front door. She was willing to patiently wait for her mother to appear.

Finally, after what seemed like an eternity, she heard her mom coming inside the house. She was barely inside when she found herself greeted by her overly anxious and enthusiastic daughter, who was apparently ready for her surprise. "Hi, Mom!" Rachel cheered. "I'm glad you're home. I've been waitin' forever!"

"Forever? . . . really?" her mom teased.

Rachel gave her a hug and talked rapidly. "Well, maybe for some minutes . . . a lot of minutes." Not waiting for her mother to bring up the surprise, Rachel thought the time was right to find out for herself. "Can we talk about the surprise?"

Her mother could see how desperately Rachel wanted to know what was going on.

She folded her arms as she thought about how much she was ready to reveal. "I think I'd rather tell you at dinner when we're all together. Just be patient. I know you're going to love what we've planned."

Rachel's eyes seemed to sparkle as she once again started to picture herself seated on her brand-new bike. After all, what else could it be? Both her mother and father knew that next to winning another Double Dutch competition, this was the only thing she wanted in the whole world. "When's dinner?" she asked.

"The same time it always is," her mom said as she began walking upstairs.

"Maybe I can start it for you," Rachel offered.

"Thank you, but I don't think you know all of what I need. But you can definitely give me a hand."

Though disappointed that she'd have to wait a little longer, Rachel went into the kitchen and waited for her mother to return and begin making dinner. Once again, she sat at the table and read the note a few more times. She hoped to find some new clues that would help her figure out the mysterious surprise.

Once her mom came into the kitchen, Rachel had little to say. All she wanted to do was help make dinner and finally find out the big mystery of the special note. She helped her mom set everything on the table and then called her dad so they could begin eating. Mr. Carter entered the kitchen, winked his eye at his wife, and sat down at the table. "I saw that," Rachel said, smiling. "I saw you winking at Mom."

Mr. Carter looked over at his wife. "I guess it's time, don't you?"

Mrs. Carter, in turn, looked over at Rachel. "Yes, I think it's time to share our good news."

Rachel wanted to close her eyes so that when her dad got up to bring in the bike she could use the expression of excitement she'd practiced in front of her mirror earlier.

"You want to start first?" Rachel's mom asked her husband.

"No, you go ahead."

Both looked lovingly at their daughter and smiled. "Well," her mom began. "We are so proud of how hard you worked to pass your final exams for the year."

"Especially your math test," her father added.

"So we decided a really special surprise was in order." Rachel's mother took a deep breath and smiled. "You're going to spend the whole summer with Uncle Walter, Aunt Marion, and your cousin Ronnie. You and Ronnie . . . I mean, Veronica . . . are the same age, but you haven't seen one another since you were infants."

Rachel sat stoic; for a moment she was unable to speak. At the sound of the words "for the whole summer," everything stopped. In one sentence, all of her plans evaporated right in front of her eyes. "But I'm gonna jump this summer with the Double Dutch Club! It was my idea, and I've been looking forward to it for months. Why can't she come here?"

"Rachel, the plans have already been made," her dad said. "They're looking forward to seeing you."

Her mom gently touched Rachel's arm. "We thought you'd be happy. Your Aunt Marion and I were so close as sisters growing up, and we want our daughters to be close too . . . understand?"

Rachel knew any attempt to protest the trip had run

out of steam even before her effort had begun. The plans were made and soon she would be on her way to Chicago to spend the summer with her relatives.

Now, on what should have been the happiest day of her life, the very last day of school, she found herself faced with the unwanted task of telling her friends some very disappointing news.

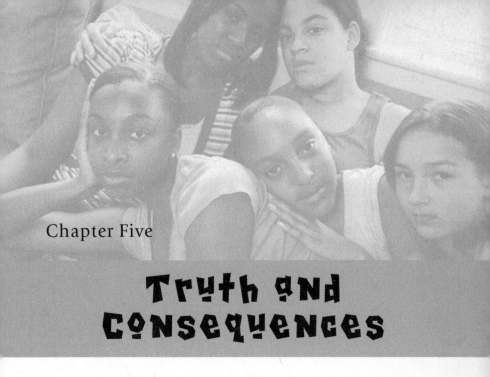

Chapter Five

Truth and Consequences

It was the last day of the school year; one that Rachel Carter had anticipated for a long time. But when her alarm sounded, instead of springing herself out of bed as she had done for the past one hundred seventy-nine days of school, she pulled the covers over her head and let out a groan of discontent. She stuck out her hand from beneath the sheet and, with her index finger, pushed the big red button on the clock to make the annoying sound stop.

When she didn't show up for breakfast, she soon

found her mother standing at the foot of her bed encouraging her to get up. "Okay, Rachel, let's go! I know you're not going to be late on the last day of the school year."

"Ughhhh . . ." she said, moaning as though in serious pain. "I don't wanna go."

Mrs. Carter was curious about Rachel's mood, but she was also a mother who knew how to choose her battles wisely. She walked over to the window directly across from her daughter's bed and opened the blinds. Bright sunshine came bursting through.

"It's beautiful out there!" she announced. "I wouldn't spend one second more in bed than I had to because I wouldn't want to miss any part of a day that looks like this one."

When Rachel didn't move, her mother then went to the window right next to the head of the bed. This time she opened the blinds *and* the window. "Listen to that," she said. "Even the birds are up greeting this gorgeous day!"

"Okay, Mom, I'm getting up." First the covers came back revealing Rachel's head.

Then slowly but surely, she emerged completely. She rubbed her eyes and walked toward the window. Gazing out at the morning sun, she thought she should feel happier.

"Good morning," her mother said cheerfully.

"Good morning," Rachel answered while asking herself on the inside, *Just how good of a morning can it really be?*

"You need to hurry, or you're going to miss the bus."

Rachel gave her mom the saddest look she could muster and hoped she might have pity on her and let her miss the last day. But as her mom left the room the only words she heard her say were, "Get ready as fast as you can."

Rachel knew that nothing about getting ready on this day was going to be easy. What should have been the sum total of a wonderful school year now made her dread even the thought of pulling herself together and making any appearance at Grover Cleveland. She was uncomfortable, and all kinds of mixed feelings were going on inside her. On the one hand, she looked forward to finishing out the last day, while at the same time she desperately wanted to hide and not tell the members of the club she was going away for the summer.

How could she tell them about this strange turn of events when she was the one responsible for initiating the idea of having the club meet in the weeks ahead to jump Double Dutch? Rachel couldn't help but feel responsible for making sure all the others committed themselves to the plan. Now it appeared as if she was going to be the lone defector and miss out on what she knew was going to be countless hours of fun.

On this morning, she took her time stepping down off the bus. Her eyes searched near the front entrance of the school for her friends; they usually walked in together. Rachel struggled with the question of how to break the news and when she should do it.

She really wanted to get it over with as soon as possible. But she also knew that when she told them the truth about her plans for the summer, there would probably be consequences.

Maybe they would ask her to leave the club and never come back. Over and over in her head she kept playing a scene of the girls of the Double Dutch Club telling her good-bye. So when she suddenly saw the others waiting up ahead, she braced herself for what she felt was going to be one of the most unpleasant situations she could ever remember having to face.

Amber was the first one to spot Rachel coming. "Hey, Rachel!" she said. Trotting some of the way to meet Rachel spelled nothing but Amber's innocent gladness. She had no clue about the coming avalanche of disappointment that Rachel's words would bring.

But soon the expression on her face changed in a few short seconds from jubilant to sad because Rachel acted as though Amber wasn't even there.

Tanya decided to find out for herself why Rachel seemed so different on this particular morning. "What's the matter with you, Rachel? 'Cause I know you heard

Amber saying hi, and you just up and ignored her."

Rachel looked at Amber and forced a smile. "I'm sorry, Amber. I was thinking about something. I didn't mean to do that."

"It's okay," Amber said, moving closer to Lindsey.

Nancy could tell something was weighing heavily on Rachel's mind, and she made an attempt to find out what it was. "You do not seem happy on this last day of school, Rachel."

"Maybe passing Mr. Whitman's test put her into some kind of shock or something," Carla suggested. "I've heard things like that can happen, but I sure wouldn't want it happening to me . . . especially today."

"So is that the problem?" Brittany inquired. "Are you in some kind of shock from passing that math test? 'Cause if you are, you need to let it go. Remember, in ten weeks we'll all be back. And next year, the math's gonna be harder."

Rachel took a deep breath. "It's not Mr. Whitman's test. I wish it was."

Lindsey was beginning to get impatient because Rachel wouldn't just tell them what was wrong. "Please just say whatever it is you want to say," she pleaded.

Rachel looked in each of their faces and hung her head slightly as though ashamed. "I won't be here."

"Won't be where?" Brittany asked.

"I can't jump this summer . . . I'm going to my cousin's in Chicago."

"I didn't know you had a cousin in Chicago," Lindsey said.

"We're the same age. My mom said we're even born in the same month. Only one day apart. She says we're like sister cousins or somethin'."

Nancy seemed relieved. "It's okay, Rachel. I believe Double Dutch is probably jumped in Chicago too."

Rachel realized that Nancy was trying to make her feel better about her dreaded news, but it did little to soften the blow she had dealt her teammates. "But I wanted to jump with all of you, and I promised I'd be here every day . . . remember?"

Rachel was surprised that Tanya wasn't giving her a hard time about her news.

"You're gonna have to practice twice as hard when you get back," she said, laughing.

Tapping her lightly on the shoulder, Tanya nodded her head. "It'll be okay."

Amber stepped forward. "We'll miss you, Rachel."

"Yeah," Lindsey echoed. "We're gonna miss you."

"We all will," added Tanya.

Rachel looked at her friends and barely kept herself from crying. She managed to show a brave smile and thought about what good friends she had and how glad she was to be a part of the Double Dutch Club. So as the girls filed into the building to begin their last day of the school year, Rachel thought about how sorry she was that she had broken her promise. She silently told herself, *I'm sure there'll be no rainbow for me this summer.*

Chapter Six

Just a Little Good-bye

The end of the last day had finally come, and Rachel waited with the rest of the girls to wish one more special someone a wonderful summer vacation. "There she is!"

Amber yelled as she hurriedly raced over to where the other girls were standing. As they watched Coach Hughes park her car, Amber tucked herself into the straight line of girls standing in single file. She positioned herself right between Lindsey and Nancy. Tanya quickly nudged Carla. "You got it?"

Since this was the fourth time she had asked that question, Carla looked more than a little annoyed. "I told you, I got it."

Tanya took a fast peek behind the line to make absolutely sure that their special gift for the coach was there. Once she saw it for herself, she felt relieved. Looking at everyone standing in line, she still had one more question. "Did everybody sign it?"

"Yes," Brittany told her. "We all signed it . . . twice!"

"Quiet!" Lindsey said, waving her hands. "Here she comes."

Coach Hughes hurried herself over to the blacktop to her awaiting team. "My, don't you all look wonderful?" She made eye contact with each and every girl standing before her. "And I know you're excited about summer vacation. Believe me," she said, "I know just how you feel."

"Really, Coach Hughes?" Carla was quick to ask. "What you gonna do for the summer?"

"I'll visit with my daughter in California."

"Does she know how to jump Double Dutch?" Amber asked.

"I don't think she jumps anymore. But Double Dutch is something that once you learn how to do it, you can jump forever, even if only in your imagination."

"What's that mean, Coach Hughes?"

"It means . . . when my daughter was a girl, she

loved jumping. But even though she's grown up now, I'll bet there are times when she closes her eyes and pictures herself back inside the ropes, jumping just like she did when she was a young girl."

Amber smiled as though pleased. "I believe it, 'cause sometimes I dream about a rope so big that we're all jumping in at the same time. You too, Coach!"

Nancy realized it was time for her to start heading home, so she gave Tanya a little nudge to let her know it was time to make their special presentation.

Amber noticed the signal and got very excited. "Now, Tanya?" she asked.

"Shush, Amber!" Lindsey told her.

But Lindsey's request went unheeded, and she persisted with her questioning.

Amber turned around and looked behind the line of girls. "Who's got it?"

The team realized there was no use in trying to hide their gift any longer. Tanya moved to the side and took one end of a large, rolled-up, bright yellow paper. She unrolled one side while Brittany unrolled the other. There in bold purple letters were the words, *HAVE A GREAT SUMMER, COACH HUGHES!* And once the banner was fully opened, the girls yelled its message out loud.

Coach Hughes was moved by the team's kind expression, and they could tell how much she loved the banner by the tears gently flowing down the sides of her face. She tried to hide them, but couldn't. The coach softly called each girl by name, gave her a hug, and graciously said thank you. And the girls were glad to know their gift meant so much to their favorite coach in the whole world.

"Thank you all so much. And I know you're going to have a great summer too!"

Carla and Rachel carefully rolled up the banner and handed it to Coach Hughes.

"I know I'll be away for the summer, but I also know seven young ladies who will probably spend every one of those days jumping and enjoying themselves."

Carla smiled. "Us, right Coach?"

"Yes, Carla. I hope you all have the best summer ever. It's good if you jump, but the important thing I want you to remember is to have fun. Have lots and lots of fun."

Brittany wasted no time answering. "Oh, we will."

"Okay, girls," said Coach Hughes as she gave each of them one more hug. "Promise me you'll enjoy yourselves while you jump."

"We promise we will," Nancy said proudly.

There it is again, Rachel thought, *that word "promise."* How good a summer could it be when she was already starting to miss her friends? Not wanting to spoil the moment, Rachel put on a fake smile, hugged everyone, and wished them all a great summer. While she may have been successful in fooling her friends, she didn't put anything over on the coach.

Coach Hughes signaled for Rachel to come near. And while Rachel readily obliged, she was careful not to let her eyes meet the eyes of her coach. She was smart enough to know that Coach Hughes had a whole lot of wisdom. One look was enough to make it seem as if she could see right through you.

And just when Rachel thought she had successfully put one over on the coach, she could tell by the tone of her voice that Coach Hughes was well aware that something was wrong. All the girls knew that Coach Hughes was never one to beat around the bush. She folded her arms and didn't move. "What's wrong, Rachel?"

For a moment Rachel considered telling her coach that everything was all right, but her good conscience prevailed and gave permission for her true feelings to come out. "I don't want to go."

"Where is it that you don't want to go?"

"To Chicago. I have to go to Chicago for the whole summer. It's not fair. And I don't want to go."

"Have you ever been there?"

Rachel wondered why the coach would ask such a question. "No," she answered softly.

"It's a beautiful city!" Coach Hughes exclaimed.

"You've been there?"

"I used to visit there all the time when I was younger. In fact, the first Double Dutch team I ever coached started in Chicago."

Rachel's eyes searched and clearly expressed that she wanted to hear more. "Did they win?"

"Oh, yes . . . they won."

"How big was the trophy?"

"Oh, they didn't win a trophy."

"But, you said . . ."

"I said they won. And they did. You always win when you try and you give your best. So I'd say that makes them winners . . . don't you?"

"Yes, Coach Hughes."

Rachel should have known that Coach Hughes would use this moment to help her learn yet another important lesson about life. "You know, Rachel," she said. "It's only good-bye for a little while. And I'm sure you're probably going to learn something special while you're in Chicago. Going to new places and meeting people can help us to grow."

Rachel surely didn't agree that ten weeks was only a *little good-bye*. "I can grow right here where I am."

"Of course you can, but I mean growing as a person. The more you learn, the better able you'll be one day to help someone else to grow."

"You mean like the way you help us with our jumping?"

"Yes, that's what I mean."

Rachel nodded her head. Deep down inside she knew Coach Hughes was right. She also knew that sometimes change doesn't come easy. This change wouldn't be easy, and she found herself feeling disappointed—and even somewhat afraid. "I'm going to miss the team while I'm gone."

"And they're going to miss you too . . . and so will I," Coach reassured her.

"But what about the promise I made to them? I said I'd jump with them every day."

"And you will." The coach leaned down to whisper. "Girls who love to jump Double Dutch never stop jumping. No matter where you are, or what your age, you will always have the ability to take a moment and allow yourself to leap inside the ropes—even if it only happens through a fond memory."

"You mean . . . like that 'jumping in your mind' thing?"

"Exactly."

Coach Hughes didn't have to say anything more. Rachel understood and gave her a big hug. "Thank you."

"I hope you have a wonderful summer, Rachel, and do some jumping for me."

"I'll try," Rachel said as she walked along with the coach. She stopped when she reached the place where the other girls were standing along the edge of the blacktop.

So while everyone waved good-bye, Coach Hughes got into her car and drove away, not to be seen again until September. Rachel tried to concentrate on everything the coach had said. But somehow she let her fears voice an opinion and suddenly found herself in mourning for a summer she knew she had already lost.

Chapter Seven

Time to Go!

The night before her trip to Chicago wasn't a comfortable one for Rachel. She tossed and turned in her bed for what seemed like hours. And with her eyes wide-open, she stared at the darkness all around her. She lay there hoping one of her parents would suddenly thrust open her door and, in a last minute reprieve, would cheerfully announce that plans for the trip had been canceled.

But Rachel knew these thoughts only amounted to wishful thinking. One quick glance over to the corner opposite her bed forced her to see the outline of her suitcases. And the sight of them caused her to frown.

How many times and in how many ways had she tried to tell her parents she didn't want to go? And why couldn't they hear her? Every time she told them how opposed she was, they'd just counteract her position by telling her how much fun she was going to have. They even encouraged her by saying they wished they were going in her place.

However, from where Rachel stood on the matter, if they were going instead of her, that wouldn't be such a bad idea. After all, her mother hadn't seen her older sister Marion in at least two years. And it had been even longer since Rachel had seen her cousin Ronnie. If it weren't for the pictures Aunt Marion sent at Christmas time each year, Rachel wouldn't know what her cousin looked like at all.

Her mom often talked about how the two children had played so nicely when they were two years old. And she had a picture to prove it. *But we're twelve now,* Rachel thought, *not two, and things have to be different.* Someone who's twelve wants to be with people who like to do what they do. *And I like Double Dutch!* she declared inwardly. But immediately following her stand on the matter, Rachel remembered that Ronnie was twelve too. And what twelve-year-old wouldn't like jumping Double Dutch? Besides, just like Rachel's mom used to jump with Aunt Marion, her aunt must have passed on those skills to her daughter. As she began painting a better picture for herself, Rachel was starting to feel a little more positive about her trip.

Since her mom and aunt had been so diligent about sending pictures and making lots of phone calls to one another, Rachel tried to convince herself that maybe her arrival wouldn't be so awkward after all. Suddenly, she felt guilty that she had never called or written to her cousin. Surely that would have made things easier. However, because so much time had passed, she didn't know what to expect.

Not wanting to think anymore, Rachel threw back the sheet and got out of bed.

She tiptoed over to her dresser and reached for the framed picture of the Double Dutch Club. It had been taken just after winning the North Carolina Jump Off. Rachel closed her eyes and smiled. She remembered what a wonderful day it had been. And for a brief moment, she was happy that she could draw from the feeling of that special moment. It was for certain one of the best and most celebrated times of her life.

She held the picture in her hand and positioned it in-line with the moonbeam that had entered her room and crisscrossed its way right above her dresser. Placing the photograph back where it belonged, Rachel got back into bed, pulled her sheet over her head, and resolved that finally it was time to face the inevitable. In the morning, her dad would come for her suitcases, load them into the car, and she would be on her way to Chicago. She knew she could go kicking and screaming, or she could go calmly and peacefully. But the one thing she knew was certain—she was going.

When she awakened the next morning, Rachel was surprised that no one had called her to come downstairs. She could hear her mother humming in the hallway outside her room. Apparently, at least one person was very happy about the trip. She kept trying to think about what Coach Hughes had said about learning new things and meeting new people. Another quick glance toward the corner in her room interrupted her thoughts and confirmed the very thing she didn't want to acknowledge. Her dad had already come and taken her suitcases and put them in the car.

Her mother opened the door and stuck her head partially inside. Rachel forced herself to welcome her with a smile. "Good morning," Rachel said as her mom turned to head downstairs.

"And good morning to you too!" her mom answered. It was a small exchange between mother and daughter, but as soon as Rachel heard her mother's humming resume, she could sense how really excited her mom was about the trip. And so she promised herself that she would try, if only for her mother's sake, to put on a good face as they prepared to leave.

Knowing she was only moments away from hearing

her father's car horn blaring, Rachel grabbed for a bowl from the kitchen cabinet, got herself a spoon from the utensil drawer, and poured herself some cereal. The second she was about to put the first spoonful in her mouth, her father walked into the room. "Time to go!" he said. For the moment he stood in front of his daughter. Just like her mom, he too was wearing a great big smile. "You're going to have a wonderful time . . . just wait and see. You and your cousin are going to have so much fun, you probably won't want to come back home."

Rachel wanted to assure her father that nothing could be further from the truth.

How could she not want to come back home when she didn't want to leave in the first place? She knew protesting at this point would serve no purpose. Both her parents looked too happy on this day. So she decided the best thing she could do was to finish her cereal as quickly as possible, keep smiling, and get into the car.

It was going to be a long ride. Rachel heard her dad tell her mom it would take close to thirteen hours to drive from New Jersey to Chicago. At least she had an ample supply of *Girls' Life* magazines, lots of her favorite music to listen to on her mp3, and a copy of *Friends to the End* by her favorite author, Millicent Vaughn. She hoped she'd have enough distractions to keep her mind occupied as she traveled such a long distance.

She checked one last time to make sure she had everything she needed. One final look inside her bag was immediately followed by a loud shout. "I gotta get something!"

Rachel's parents were just about to get into the car when she bolted out of the backseat.

With her key in hand, she raced for the front door. Then in less than three minutes later she was back at the car holding the one thing she'd almost forgotten. It was her Double Dutch ropes. "Now, I'm ready," she said panting while carefully placing the long, folded ropes in her bag.

Rachel's mom turned around and smiled. "You and Ronnie are going to have so much fun jumping this summer. Just the way your Aunt Marion and I used to do."

"I hope so," Rachel answered nestling herself comfortably in the backseat of the car. Staring out the window, she silently repeated her thoughts. *I hope so.*

Chapter Eight

Arrival

Rachel's dad had been correct almost right down to the number of minutes it had taken them to drive to Chicago. It took exactly twelve hours and thirty-eight minutes. But if anyone had asked Rachel, she would have said it felt like it took twenty hours.

Upon finally arriving in the place she had heard referred to as "The Windy City," she took a deep breath and stared out the window. "Hmmpf," she said, sticking her finger out of the car as though testing the air. "I don't feel any wind at all." However, she was amazed at the sight of the beautiful skyline that appeared as though it stretched completely across the sky and extended itself over the city.

"Where do they live? And how long will it take us to get there from here?" She said, intentionally trying to sound anxious and excited. *After all,* she told herself, *there is definitely no chance of going back now.* The least she could try and do was give her parents the impression she was looking forward to her visit.

"We're just about there," her father assured her. "They live over on Euclid Street. It's pretty nice. You'll see."

Nice? Rachel thought. As far as she was concerned, nice was back home in New Jersey where she'd left her good friends.

Within minutes, her dad was pulling up in front of a well-kept, red brick, two-story home on a street where every other home pretty much looked the same. There were some with neatly trimmed hedges, while others were adorned with multicolored rosebushes. But all had one thing in common. They each had a small, well-kept front yard with nicely manicured green grass. "There it is!" Rachel's mother said pointing at the address. She spoke with a sweet melody in her voice. It was the voice Rachel knew her mother used when she was happy. "I think I see Ronnie outside!" Excitedly, she pointed toward a group of girls. "That's her! That's her!"

There was a small group of three girls playing what looked like hopscotch out in front of the brick house. Mrs. Carter hurried and powered down her window.

"Ronnie!" she yelled, partially sticking her head out the window to make sure the girls heard her and to give herself a better view. Rachel stared in amazement and found herself wanting to shrink from what she felt was a total embarrassment. She had never seen her mother act this way before. Besides it reminded her of someone she knew quite well. It reminded her of herself. For the first time in her life, Rachel realized that she could picture her mother as a twelve-year-old. She wondered if one day some years from now she would be as giddy and excited to see her cousin Ronnie again.

Suddenly she watched her mom's joy turn to disappointment. When Mr. Carter steered the car close enough for Mrs. Carter to see clearly, she saw that none of the girls playing out front was her beloved niece Ronnie.

Rachel's dad was careful to take another look at the street sign to make sure they had arrived at the right place. "You did say they live at 233 Euclid, right?"

"No, I said 323."

Rachel's dad had that expression he often made when he knew why something didn't happen the way it was supposed to. It was the same look he'd have when he'd searched in the refrigerator for the butter, but couldn't find it because someone had pushed it all the way to the back. Though, just like then, he didn't complain. He'd just move it up to the front until the next time when he would have "that look," which said he was searching for it again. He just inhaled a little bit and continued looking for the right address. "Well, that just means we've got a little farther to go," he said.

Carefully, he drove the car back into the main part of the street and continued on until he spotted a house that began with the number three hundred. This time, when he pulled up in front of the house with the numbers 323, he was certain he was at the right address.

"That's it," Mrs. Carter said pointing at the brick front two-story home. You could hear the happiness had once again returned in her voice. Rachel smiled at her dad, and he smiled back. It was their own little way of expressing how glad they were that this time they had found the right place. "That's really it!" Mrs. Carter said with 100 percent certainty.

Maybe it was out of desperation, but Rachel decided to make one last attempt to get out of her planned summer vacation. "What if they're not home? Can we turn around and go back to New Jersey?"

Neither of her parents answered but instead gave her the "other look" that said she had reached her destination and would remain until the end of August.

Mr. Carter spotted someone pulling out of a parking space only three cars away from their relatives' front door. That made him as happy as he remembered he had been when he was a young boy opening one of his Christmas gifts. Mrs. Carter wasted no time getting out of the car. For the first few moments she just stood on the sidewalk and took in all of the sights around her.

Rachel noticed how quickly the people she saw were moving about; watching them reminded her of her trip to New York. People moved from place to place quickly there too, and it made her wonder if that was the way life was in all cities.

Mrs. Carter thought about how much she had missed the sounds of the city from the summers of her girlhood. She remembered counting cars with her sister, Marion, and playing rope games out in front of her house until it got dark. And she recalled how easy it used to be to visit her grandma who only lived five houses up in the next block. The building where Nanna used to live had been torn down years ago. But when Mrs. Carter gazed across the street, she could still see her grandma sitting in her favorite chair and insisting that she and Marion "help themselves" to some creamy homemade vanilla ice cream.

The sound of a horn being blown by a passing car immediately caused that familiar scene from the past to disappear from sight. "C'mon, Rachel, let's start walking. They live right there," she said as she pointed at a well-kept brownstone with large bay windows on either side.

As they walked toward the home, Rachel and her mom each carried a small bag while her dad juggled the two larger suitcases. Before they reached the steps, a tall, husky man and a woman whose beautifully braided hair draped neatly about her shoulders met them halfway. Walking slowly and almost cautiously behind them was a pretty twelve-year-old girl who, though she would probably reject the idea, slightly resembled Rachel. But it only took one glance to see they were similar in height, weight, and even shared the same honey-colored complexion. As soon as she spotted them, Mrs. Carter, who for that moment became twelve again, shouted and screamed with excitement, "Marion! Marion!"

While she was calling her sister's name, Aunt Marion did exactly the same thing. "I see you, Carol!" she hollered. "I see all of you!" And when the two sisters reached each other, Mrs. Carter let go of the bag she was carrying, causing it to fall to the ground. Then she lovingly threw her arms around her sister's neck. Rachel and her father stood on the sidewalk watching the two sisters as they began their own long-awaited little family reunion right there in the middle of Euclid Street.

"Okay, you two," Uncle Walter bellowed. "Let's at least try to make it into the house before you get all emotional."

Mr. Carter laughed and shook his head agreeably. He knew it was no use trying to separate two sisters who hadn't given each other a hug in close to two years.

Uncle Walter patted Mr. Carter on the back, reached

out his hand, and took one of the suitcases. As the two men began walking toward the house, Rachel smiled because she liked the sound of her uncle's voice. It was rich and deep; when he laughed, it sounded so warm and friendly—you couldn't help but feel welcomed.

Though it wasn't easy, Rachel's mom and aunt let go of each other just long enough for her mom to retrieve the bag she'd dropped to the ground. So with bags in hand, they also began to walk toward the warm and inviting home. Now the only two people left standing on the sidewalk were Rachel and her cousin Ronnie, whom she hadn't seen since they were toddlers. One studied the other, but neither spoke. Rachel wondered what she could say to begin a conversation. She remembered how Coach Hughes would always tell the girls that "being friendly was the easiest way to make a new friend." Rachel thought it was advice worth trying.

"It's kinda nice here," Rachel said, deliberately leaving an opening for her cousin to get into the conversation. To her surprise, instead of a warm response, she was met with a stiff, cold stare from Ronnie, whose attitude clearly said, *Leave me alone, because you're annoying me.* In spite of getting the message, Rachel decided to try again. After all, she'd learned along with her friends in the Double Dutch Club that many of the things in life worth achieving sometimes wouldn't be easy. *Ronnie is family,* she told herself, *so that means it's worth trying a little harder to be friends.*

The very second Rachel had made up her mind to offer another olive branch of peace, Ronnie decided to speak. "How long you gonna be here?" she demanded. There was no mistaking her intent. She considered Rachel a major inconvenience and possibly even her greatest rival.

These were not the words Rachel had expected to hear. So she found herself unsure about how to answer. "My mom said I'd be staying for the summer."

Upon hearing that, Ronnie's cold demeanor fell a few more degrees. "Whattya mean, the whole summer?" she asked. "I've got things to do, and I don't have time to babysit you." Rachel was offended but decided not to complain. She knew she didn't need anyone to babysit her, least of all someone who probably couldn't even take care of herself. They were the same age, after all. Ronnie's voice was so loud, Rachel was sure everyone in the entire neighborhood must have heard her question.

Knowing she deserved no response, Rachel went ahead and gave her one anyway.

"Yes," she said softly, "the whole summer." And at the sound of the word *summer,* Rachel immediately felt trapped.

Rachel knew it was ridiculous to think that her

cousin might offer to help her carry her bag into the house, but she hoped Ronnie might suggest it. Instead, she started walking ahead of Rachel toward her home. She stopped for a second, turned around, and once again rolled her eyes. "Well, you might as well c'mon."

Rachel thought about how sad she had felt when she found out she'd be leaving her friends in New Jersey and how she didn't want to go to Chicago in the first place.

But now she realized something that hadn't occurred to her before. It was pretty clear; her cousin Ronnie didn't want her to come to Chicago either.

As she slowly walked to the place where she was going to spend the twelfth summer of her life, Rachel tried to fill her mind with thoughts of meeting new people and learning to do some of the new things Coach Hughes had talked about. She stopped and closed her eyes, desiring to concentrate on something good.

But in all of those thoughts, no matter how much she tried to block the negative ones from getting through, the one that kept nagging at her as she trudged up the steps to go inside was, *How am I going to get through the next two months living with someone who wished I'd never come?*

Chapter Nine

Name Game

Rachel felt a little better knowing her parents were going to stay the night and rest so they could get a fresh start driving back early the next morning. She worried about how things would be once they were gone. But she also felt a tiny bit more at ease just knowing she had the rest of the day with them and at least one more night.

Unfortunately, it was a night that came and was gone all too quickly, and in what seemed like a flash. Mr. and Mrs. Carter hugged their daughter and got into the car to begin their long drive home.

"Be good," Mrs. Carter encouraged while giving

Rachel a great big hug, then gently placing her hands on Rachel's shoulders. "You're going to have a real good time."

Rachel forced a smile, nodded her head, and squeezed her mom warmly. When her father held out his arms, she walked over to give him a hug too. "We're going to miss you," he told her. "So don't you go off and forget who we are."

Rachel looked up at her father and smiled. "I won't."

"Promise?"

Rachel hesitated because she knew making a promise carried a lot of meaning—especially with her dad. Maybe if she didn't answer his question, her parents wouldn't leave her. Perhaps they would realize they couldn't bear the thought of not seeing their daughter every day for the next two months. And once they came to their senses, they would insist that she get into the car, and they'd all happily go back home where they belonged. But those were only thoughts floating around in Rachel's head. And the moment she heard her father calling her name, she awakened from her daydream.

"Rachel? Did you hear me?"

"Yes, Daddy, I promise I won't forget you and Mom." Now she had spoken the words that gave her mom and dad permission to say good-bye. The sad part, though, was in knowing she'd made a promise that had no way of bringing about any rainbows. She thought of the beautiful rainbow she'd seen that day of the storm. *Rainbows,* she told herself, *are reminders of good things to come.* And as hard as Rachel tried to picture something good coming out of her stay in Chicago, right now, all she could see was the storm clouds forming overhead. From where she stood, the picture before her was that of her cousin Ronnie wearing a scowl of discontent, and there was absolutely nothing good about that.

"I won't forget you," she repeated. Although when she said it this time, she wasn't sure whose benefit she was saying it for—her parents or her own.

Mr. Carter hugged his daughter again, "I know you won't."

"Well, if your father gets another hug, then so do I," her mother said jokingly. Aunt Marion, Uncle Walter, and Ronnie walked over and hugged them good-bye as well.

Rachel gave her mother one last hug, put on a brave face, and watched her parents get into the car and slowly pull away. Within a few short seconds they were absorbed in the busy Chicago traffic and disappeared from sight. She held up her hand and continued waving long after she couldn't see them anymore. And when she turned around, there standing behind her were her aunt, her uncle, and the cousin she was somehow going to have to learn to get along with for the next two months.

Though there may have been a slight resemblance, Rachel suddenly realized the only thing she and Ronnie seemed to have in common was the fact that they were both twelve. Rachel inspected herself and her cousin from head to toe, trying to find something similar that would connect them as family.

Rachel wore her hair in a ponytail, because it was comfortable when she was jumping Double Dutch. Ronnie's hair was curled and flipped on the ends. Rachel wore a T-shirt, jeans, and sneakers, while her cousin wore designer jeans, sneakers, and a cute pink polo. Since her clothes were spotless, she probably didn't welcome the idea of taking part in anything that might result in her getting dirty. So the more Rachel studied her, the more she came to conclude that her cousin probably didn't jump Double Dutch at all. Shaking her head, she whispered, "Bet she couldn't jump her way over a short bush even if she had help."

In spite of the disappointment she was feeling with her parents gone, Rachel knew if she ever planned to start getting to know Ronnie, the time was now. "So, whatya wanna do?" she asked.

Ronnie's smile was smug and almost had a slyness about it. "How about I invite some of my friends over? I know they'd want to meet you."

Finally, Rachel thought. *I get to meet some other kids, and maybe they'll want to jump rope.*

"C'mon," Ronnie ordered while waving her hand for Rachel to follow.

"I'm comin'. Wait up, Ronnie," Rachel said struggling to keep up with her cousin who was purposefully walking really fast. Suddenly, and without warning, she turned around. And when she did, she made sure she stared directly into Rachel's eyes. "Don't you ever call me Ronnie!" She demanded. "My name is Veronica!"

Rachel was stunned and for a few seconds found herself unable to move. *What was the big deal?* she asked herself. *Maybe I should tell her to call me Rachel Nicole.*

Rachel couldn't remember what her cousin was like when they were younger, but was pretty sure she had to have been a whole lot better than this stranger who played a peculiar name game and demanded she be called Veronica. It was irritating that she didn't know anything about the girl walking just a few steps ahead of her—a girl who wasn't very friendly and who obviously didn't know the first thing about making a guest feel welcome. The best thing to do, she resolved, was to call her by the name she preferred. "Sure, Veronica," she conceded. "No problem."

After all, she was staying in Veronica's home, and there was still a long summer ahead. The idea of having Veronica as an enemy gave Rachel a queasy feeling in the pit of her stomach—and she didn't like it. So inwardly she vowed to do her best to try and get along with a girl who, if she had any likable qualities, was doing an exceptional job at keeping them very well hidden.

Walking behind her cousin, Rachel followed her inside to finish her breakfast. When Veronica reached the top step, she turned around and peered down at Rachel. "Oh, and when you meet my friends, don't say nothing stupid!" With that said, she went inside and never turned around to see the hurt look that had landed on Rachel's face. In that moment, she wished her parents would come back and give her one more hug just to reassure her that everything would be all right. But the reality was that they weren't coming back any time soon. So she had to accept the fact that she was now on Veronica's turf, and that was a place where Rachel Carter had no vote.

It was obvious that things were going to be done Veronica's way or no way at all.

Rachel felt trapped. And this feeling was even worse than the time she and her dad had been stuck in an elevator at the First Avenue Bank downtown. When that incident happened, at least the newspapers ran a story and a picture showing them when they finally got out.

Though it had been a frightening experience, Rachel felt like a celebrity when everyone at school saw the picture in the local paper. *And that whole thing,* she reminded herself, *only lasted for fifteen minutes.* There was no comparing the two situations. *In fact,* she told herself, *being stuck in an elevator rather than having to be bossed around by Veronica looks a whole lot better than the way I feel right now.*

Rachel wanted Veronica to like her, and she wanted to like her cousin too. But the idea of the two of them becoming friends didn't seem likely. *After all,* she thought, *friends you can pick and choose, but relatives are your relatives no matter what.*

As soon as they got inside, they sat down at the table to finish breakfast. It was still very early, and there was plenty of time to plan the day. "What kinds of things do you do here in the summer?" Rachel asked.

Veronica was swift with her answer. "Better things than I bet you do in New Jersey." Rachel wondered why every word out of her cousin's mouth had to be so harsh and insulting. None of it made any sense. If she was trying to make Rachel dislike her, she was quickly succeeding. Rachel figured it would do her no good to complain, because every time Veronica let her bad attitude show, her parents were nowhere around to see it. As far as they were concerned, Veronica was their little princess.

Rachel thought about how often Coach Hughes encouraged the team to keep trying no matter how difficult something appeared. So she again attempted to break through what started out as a manageable piece of ice but was now quickly turning into a full-fledged iceberg. And the hardest part about tackling it was in knowing it had successfully settled itself between the two of them.

"You jump?" Rachel asked. Hoping to hear her say yes would allow her to excuse her cousin's unfriendly behavior. She waited for Veronica to answer; but instead of saying something, she gave her that "are you kidding me?" look again, rolled her eyes, and took a big bite out of the piece of toast she was eating. Rachel decided to be more persistent. "I said, do you JUMP?"

She didn't seem the least bit interested but did answer. "Jump what?"

"Double Dutch . . . do you jump?"

Veronica laughed. "I do pageants, and so do all of my friends."

"Pageants . . . ? You mean like . . ."

"Yes, beauty pageants. In fact, I almost won Little Miss Chicago a couple of months ago."

"You were first runner-up?"

"No."

"Second runner-up? . . . third?"

Veronica was annoyed by Rachel's questions. "Since you want to be so nosey, I'll tell you. I didn't place, but I will next time."

Rachel saw this as an opportunity to do a little boasting of her own. "Our Double Dutch team took first place in the North Carolina Jump Off a coupla months ago. You should see the trophy," she said, raising her hand as high as her head to help Veronica get a clear picture of its size.

It would have been too easy for Veronica to just offer her congratulations and leave it at that. "Nobody cares about that stupid jump rope stuff!" She huffed, got up from her seat, and left the room.

And Rachel fired back. "WELL, NOBODY CARES ABOUT THOSE STUPID PAGEANTS EITHER!"

"And I wish you hadn't come here!" Veronica shouted.

"And I wish I didn't come here either!"

Rachel stood alone in the kitchen feeling worse than ever. She thought of how her father had often reminded her about how easy it was to be nice to others when they're nice to us, but how difficult it was to be nice to someone who was mean or cruel to us in return. This, he would tell her, was a true test of our character. Rachel gazed toward the stairs and then hung her head, realizing that she had just failed that very test.

Nooo Problem

Aunt Marion hurried into the kitchen to see what all the noise was about. "What's going on?" she asked. "I could hear shouting all the way upstairs."

Rachel wanted to tell just how awfully mean Veronica was being to her. But when she looked at her aunt, so much about her reminded her of her mom that she couldn't bring herself to do it. She could see how they shared the same kindness in their eyes and a pleasant smile that could warm up any room they entered. So she totally dismissed the idea of exposing Veronica for being a terrible hostess and a horrible cousin. "Nothing, Aunt Marion," she said. "Everything's okay. We were trying to make up our minds about what to do today. And I guess we got a little too loud. Sorry."

Without anyone noticing, Veronica suddenly and very quietly reentered the kitchen. "Me too, Mom . . . sorry about the noise."

Aunt Marion looked carefully at Veronica and then at Rachel. Neither girl said another word, but they could sense she didn't fully believe them. However, both were relieved that she had accepted their explanation. Aunt Marion shared how she and Rachel's mom used to have some of the loudest shouting matches. Then after a few minutes had passed, they were closer than ever and soon trying to find something fun to do together. *After all*, Rachel thought, *that's the way sisters are.*

"You two remind me of my sister and me," she said, shaking her head. "And take it from me, nobody was closer than we were as girls growing up. Trust me. By the end of the summer, you'll see what I mean."

Once Veronica knew she was in the clear, she left the room. Rachel remained and hoped her aunt wouldn't notice how troubled she was because she knew that she and Veronica would never get along the way her mom and Aunt Marion had. "What made you so close?" She asked her aunt, hoping she'd reveal some helpful hints.

"A lot of things, I guess," Aunt Marion said. "I was older, so I usually tried to be the boss. I wanted her to play my games, my way, my time."

Rachel's eyes widened. She tried to imagine her mother as a girl of twelve. "And my mom? Did she go along with whatever you said?"

"Most of the time she did. I think it made her feel good when she knew I was happy. I think she's still like that. That's one reason why I love her so. She can be happy just because someone else is happy."

Rachel knew what Aunt Marion was saying was true. She'd seen that happiness all her life. If she shared good news about her school day with her mom, her mother would light up as if she had been there experiencing it all with her.

"The other reason why I think she would play the games I wanted was because she was my baby sister and she knew I loved her. Every time she'd agree to do something the way I wanted it done, it only made me change my mind and let her decide. So we both kind of got our way. Her kindness made me want to be kind too . . . know what I mean?"

"Yeah, I do." As fast as Rachel answered her aunt's question, she wondered if Veronica would ever be willing to compromise. In fact, she wondered if the word "compromise" was even part of her vocabulary.

"Your Uncle Walter and I have to run a few errands. It's early, so we'll be back in time enough to take you girls to an afternoon movie. While we're gone, I want you and Veronica to straighten up the kitchen."

Rachel was certain it wasn't going to be easy to get Veronica to do her part, but she didn't put up any resistance. "Sure, Aunt Marion," she replied. "No problem."

"We won't be gone long." Aunt Marion said as she kissed Rachel on the cheek. She then hurried out the door to meet Uncle Walter who was waiting in the car in front of their home.

Rachel thought of how Coach Hughes always said if you want to get something over and done with, start tackling the task as early as possible. Rachel looked at the pile of dirty dishes waiting in the sink and decided the time to start was now. All she needed to do was get Veronica downstairs to do her part. Rachel perched herself at the bottom of the stairs, leaned her head back, and yelled in her loudest voice. "Ronnie! Come down here and help me!"

By the time she had said the word "me," her cousin came charging out of her room and back down the stairs. Rachel gave a sigh of relief because she thought Veronica was going to do the right thing and pitch in with cleaning up. But she was wrong. Veronica saw this as another opportunity to taunt Rachel. Again she rolled her eyes and said in the meanest voice, "I told you to call me Veronica." Then she mumbled a few more words, turned around, and headed back up the stairs.

Rachel wasn't going to let her get away this time, so she spoke quickly. "Aunt Marion said she wanted *us* to clean up the kitchen. You're supposed to help too."

Without a thought or a comment, Veronica never looked back. She ascended the stairs like a queen stepping toward her throne. And when she reached the top, she yelled down to Rachel, "You do 'em," and slammed her door.

Rachel tried to draw strength from the voices of her mother and Coach Hughes. She could hear them reminding her over and over again, "To make a friend, you have to be friendly." And while she had no disagreement with their advice, she realized they hadn't told her what to do when being friendly didn't work. Walking back into the kitchen, she looked at the messy dishes and began filling the sink with hot sudsy water. She didn't move until each and every breakfast dish had been washed, dried, and neatly put away.

When her aunt and uncle returned, Rachel could see they were pleased with the job she'd done. As if on cue, Veronica came sauntering down the stairs like she had just been announced as the grand winner in one of her beauty pageants. "You girls did an excellent job!" Uncle Walter praised. "This is at least worth a triple scoop after the movie. Be ready to name your flavors!"

Rachel could tell by the smile on Aunt Marion's face that she was equally satisfied with what she saw. "It's beautiful! And I love the way you girls are working together. It's me and your mother all over again," she said proudly as she looked at Rachel.

Hearing how happy her aunt and uncle were with the way the kitchen turned out and seeing Veronica share in the credit only poured salt into an already aching wound. But Rachel knew a tough spot when she saw one. And this was a real tough spot to be in.

Now, she told herself, *I know what it feels like to be one of those wishbones Dad and I enjoy breaking when we have roast turkey or chicken for dinner. It hurts, and this is so unfair. How dare Veronica take credit for all the work I did?* Rachel was feeling a push from the inside that was forcing the words "She didn't help" to leave the tip of her tongue. Just as she was planning to shout it out as loudly as possible, it became impossible when Rachel saw how happy her aunt and uncle were. So once again, she decided not to tell.

As soon as she had made her decision to remain quiet, she could feel something crack on the inside— just like that wishbone. Rachel knew in this incident she had gotten the shorter piece, so that made her the loser in the match. She wasn't going to be the one to spoil the picture her aunt had created of the two cousins working together and enjoying one another's company.

"You girls hurry up," Uncle Walter urged. "The movie starts at one."

Rachel almost went back on her own vow of silence when she saw Veronica make that sly grin and roll her eyes. "Okay, Daddy," she said sweetly polishing her words with tons of politeness.

"You too, Rachel," Aunt Marion cheered. "Hope you're ready to go."

"Yes, I'm ready," Rachel said softly. Remembering what her parents had taught her about being respectful when you're a guest in someone's home convinced Rachel she had done the right thing by not telling on Veronica. But when she dared to think about all the days of summer that were yet to come, she knew if those days could be over in one night, time still couldn't move fast enough for her.

Chapter Eleven

The Luncheon

Rachel had never seen three weeks move as slowly as the first three she'd spent with her Aunt Marion, Uncle Walter, and her first cousin Veronica. She found herself amazed that after exactly twenty-one days, nine hours, and fifteen minutes, she still hadn't met any of Veronica's friends. Every time she tried to bring up the matter, Veronica would dismiss it by saying, "Maybe tomorrow." So by day twenty-two, Rachel made up her mind to get some answers.

The first place she found herself was at Veronica's door, convinced that she could muster up the courage to knock. When she felt ready, that first knock, which had gone unanswered, then became a loud bang. When she still didn't answer, Rachel started calling her. "Ronnie! I mean, Veronica," she called. "Answer the door!" The second she started thinking there was no use in trying to talk to her, the door slowly crept open. "Whatya want?" a sleepy looking Veronica questioned.

"I wanna meet some of your friends today. You said I would, but so far I ain't met none of 'em. You got friends . . . right?"

"Maybe tomorrow," Veronica offered and began slowly closing her door. Rachel quickly stuck her foot in the way so the door couldn't close. This was the same thing she had been told last week and the week before that. This time, however, Rachel refused to accept her cousin's answer. She was serious about wanting to meet some of Veronica's friends. "TODAY," she demanded.

Veronica tried to ignore the look of determination on Rachel's face.

"I said . . ." Veronica started.

"I heard what you said, but I said today!" It was pretty clear that Rachel was tired of acting civil to someone who had such little regard for her feelings. She knew if the shoe had been on the other foot, her parents would have never allowed her to treat Veronica the way she had been treated.

Veronica wasn't used to Rachel challenging her or standing up to her in any way. And this time, she didn't seem as confident as she had on the day Rachel arrived at her home. Suddenly, she was just a twelve-year-old girl who no longer appeared as tough as she presented herself to be. "I'll ask my mother if it's okay to call so they can come over later." Rachel moved her foot out of the way. And without saying another word, Veronica closed her door.

Rachel walked away feeling like she'd won a small victory. Maybe there was still time to salvage what, up to this point, looked like a disastrous summer. Finally, she was going to meet some of Veronica's friends. "Good," Rachel said as she turned around and went down the stairs. "Maybe now I'll get to have some fun."

Aunt Marion was pleased that Veronica had asked if she could invite some of her friends over. Rachel was also glad that she followed through and called three girls and asked them to come around twelve-thirty. Aunt Marion encouraged Rachel and Veronica and said she would help them to prepare a nice lunch for the girls so it could be like a celebration. Rachel loved the idea, but she noticed her cousin wasn't very excited.

Nevertheless, they covered the table with a pretty powder blue tablecloth and placed on top of it colorful pink cups, napkins, plates, and silverware for five.

Rachel hadn't felt this good since the last day of school right before the start of summer vacation. And although she didn't expect that spending the afternoon with Veronica's friends to be anything like the great times she always had with the Double Dutch Club, she happily anticipated their arrival just the same. She stepped around the table one more time to make sure everything was *just so.*

"What do ya think?" she asked Veronica.

Without really looking at the beautiful table setting, Veronica gave a halfhearted response. "It's all right, I guess."

Rachel was determined not to allow Veronica to spoil this afternoon the way she had managed to do every day for the past three weeks. The minute everything was set up for their guests, Veronica began walking toward the stairs.

"Where ya going?" Rachel asked. "They're gonna be here in a coupla minutes!"

"When they get here, I'll be back!" she snapped.

As soon as Veronica reached the top of the stairs, Rachel heard the doorbell ringing.

"See!" she said excitedly running to answer the door. "Ya might as well come on back, 'cause they're here!"

Veronica heard the doorbell, but acted as if she didn't. The second Rachel opened the door, she could hear Veronica's door closing. "I don't care," she said gripping her hand around the doorknob.

"She's not gonna mess up this day," Rachel declared.

She thrust open the door and found the first guest for the afternoon, wearing an enormous smile. It was Marguerita Lopez, and she was as anxious as Rachel for the fun-filled afternoon to get under way. She had only lived in the neighborhood for a short time but seemed to have a real knack for making new friends. From the very first day her family moved into their home, the minute their belongings were all inside, Marguerita walked up to a group of children playing on the sidewalk and gave them a big "hello." Everyone who knew her agreed, there wasn't a shy bone in her body. If she wanted to know something, she'd ask. And from her first day in the neighborhood, she declared herself to be Veronica's new "best friend." It wasn't unusual for her to visit unannounced, but after ten visits or so of being ignored, she decided to give up and hadn't been back since.

Rachel was glad to see a new face and welcomed Marguerita inside. "Come in," she said waving her hand. "Hi! My name's Rachel. I'm Veronica's cousin, and I usually live in New Jersey, but I came to Chicago for the summer."

"I'm Marguerita," she said, entering the small hallway positioned perpendicular from the kitchen. "My grandma lives in New Jersey. I've been there a coupla times to see her."

"Did ya like it?"

"I wasn't there too long, but I guess it was okay."

Marguerita walked in behind Rachel and entered the kitchen. "You can sit here," Rachel told her as she pointed to a chair. "Where's everybody else?"

Marguerita was surprised by Rachel's question. "Everybody else?"

"Yeah, two more of Veronica's friends are coming."

"I don't think so."

Rachel resolved that Marguerita couldn't have been more wrong. And though she seemed friendly enough, surely she didn't know Veronica as well as she thought she did.

"Oh, they'll be here," Rachel said confidently. "They're Veronica's good friends."

As if by reflex, to keep from looking into Rachel's eyes, Marguerita bowed her head.

"What's wrong?" Rachel inquired softly.

"Those girls aren't comin' . . . just me."

Rachel shook her head no as though refusing to hear what Marguerita was trying to tell her. This was, after all, a luncheon put together by her beautiful, popular, overly confident cousin Veronica who was never at a loss for words and certainly couldn't be at a loss for friends. "Whataya mean, just you?"

"They used to come, but after a while they just stopped. She was always so mean to everybody. They kinda got tired of the way she treated them and just stopped coming. And Veronica stopped asking them to."

"But you came."

"My mom said I should even though Veronica wasn't nice to me either. She's been like that ever since she got real sick last year."

Rachel's eyes widened with interest. "What do ya mean sick? When was Veronica sick?"

"She was very sick . . . in the hospital and everything . . . heard my mother say it was some kind of anemia. I don't know what that is, but it's got something to do with the blood. She missed most of last school year. And it was when she came back that all that talk about pageants got started. I think when she lost her hair, she didn't think she was pretty no more."

Rachel was stunned by the news Marguerita had shared. She suddenly realized the neatly styled hairdo Veronica wore to perfection wasn't her hair at all. It was a daily reminder of almost a year's worth of illness. "But she said all of you were in pageants too."

"None of us are," Marguerita said softly. "And from what I heard, Veronica's never been in one either. I think she got embarrassed when everybody found out she was lying. Now she just pretends she's busy and doesn't have time for any of us. When she called, I thought maybe something had changed, but I can tell it hasn't. The other times when I tried to come over, she'd say she wasn't feeling well and didn't want any company."

Rachel suddenly had a peculiar look. "You know anything about beauty pageants?"

"No . . . nothin'."

"Maybe we should find out about them. Maybe we should have a pageant of our own." Rachel could tell by the expression on Marguerita's face that she was more than willing to try and wanted to hear more.

"Our own beauty pageant?"

"Yeah, we can put it together ourselves and maybe offer some kinda prize for the winner. Or maybe we should just have it for fun." Rachel thought for a moment. "I do have a question."

Marguerita smiled. "What's that?"

"Do you and the girls who didn't show up know anything about jumping Double Dutch?"

"I'm not sure about them, but I do!" Marguerita said enthusiastically. She looked as if she expected an answer because she could tell Rachel knew a question was coming. "But what's jumping Double Dutch got to do with a beauty pageant?"

"Oh, you'll see," Rachel said confidently. "Just wait. . . . think Veronica will want to be in it?"

"I dunno. Maybe. I think she's really afraid of getting laughed at. There was this girl at school who went around telling everybody she was a good singer and pretty soon it was all over the whole school. So when we had an assembly, the principal asked her to sing 'The Star Spangled Banner.' And when she got up to sing, it was so bad and so many kids was laughin' that after that she wouldn't sing no more. I don't think Veronica wants that to happen to her."

"It won't," Rachel assured her. "I know what it's like when you feel you're being pulled away from your friends and you can't do nothing about it. It's not a good feeling. Maybe when Veronica got sick that's how she felt . . . like being sick was pullin' her away from all of you."

Marguerita nodded her head yes. "Ya know something else?"

"What's that?"

"I don't think Veronica even believes she's pretty enough to win a beauty pageant."

Without any warning, Rachel found herself defending her cousin. "She is, you know."

"Huh?"

"She's pretty enough to win a hundred contests."

"I know she is," Marguerita agreed softly.

The two girls waited patiently, hoping Veronica would come out of her room and return for what they believed could still be a fun afternoon. Close to an hour had passed when Marguerita decided to give up and go home.

The minute Rachel closed the door she headed upstairs

to take a good look at her cousin. Maybe she hadn't seen the way Veronica really was because she was blinded by her bad attitude and the constant sarcasm in her voice. Maybe a closer look was exactly what she needed to help break through the great barrier Veronica had carefully crafted around herself.

Rachel trudged up the stairs. With every step she took, she thought about what she was going to say. With her hand on the doorknob, she began turning it slowly. Quietly she opened the door and stepped inside. Remembering all the bad things she had wanted to say to Veronica made Rachel feel remorseful. She could see Veronica sitting on the bed with her back facing the door. She was whimpering like a small child. And for the first time, Rachel could see that the mean-spirited exterior she wore was simply a small fort of protection she had created around her heart.

Veronica wasn't a beauty pageant winner at all; just a little girl who seemed frightened and alone. She missed the friends who no longer came around because they had been pushed away too many times. And when they left, so did all the laughter and the fun. Rachel no longer felt dislike for her cousin. Instead, she could feel herself beginning to understand her. Veronica believed she had to win a contest to be beautiful, but Rachel wanted her to know she already possessed beauty. She just needed a way to help her to see it for herself.

So, for a brief moment, standing in the doorway of her cousin's room, Rachel put herself in Veronica's place. She didn't fully understand why her cousin acted the way she did but believed if she could help her feel good about herself again and get her friends back, everyone would see a Veronica who was better than ever.

Rachel wished the girls of the Double Dutch Club were there with her. *If they were here,* she told herself, *they'd know what to do.* Accepting the fact that they weren't there made Rachel remember who was. She thought of the storm again and remembered the rainbow. And more than the rainbow, she remembered the promise. She could hear her father reminding her, "God is always with us."

Knowing she wasn't alone gave her the strength she needed to face her cousin. She stepped fully inside Veronica's room and quietly sat down on the bed beside her. She gently took her cousin's hands, bowed her head, and prayed. When she finished her prayer, she saw that Veronica had tears in her eyes. She looked at Rachel and smiled. Rachel, in turn, put her arms around her and moved closer. "It's okay," she said. "It's okay."

Chapter Twelve

A Lesson Learned

Listening to Marguerita made Rachel realize that she had judged Veronica unfairly. And knowing this made her want to do something to make things right. Later that day as she sat in the kitchen, she remembered the time she had taken an awful fall from her bike and had broken her left arm. Putting the physical pain aside, she recalled the worst part of all was the fact that she couldn't jump Double Dutch for six weeks.

On the way to the hospital she feared she might die, but the fear left her when she awakened to find her father kneeling beside her bed whispering a prayer for her healing. Feeling strength from the words her father spoke to God on her behalf helped Rachel see the importance of putting her trust in God's power.

This was one of those lessons Coach Hughes was always trying to instill in the girls on the team. She was quick to tell them, "Never judge anyone without knowing the 'whole story.'" Then she'd say, "And once you have the whole story, you still can't judge. Leave that to the only one who has that right." Rachel knew Coach Hughes meant God. So right there in her aunt's kitchen, she told God she was sorry and prayed that Veronica would forgive her.

When Rachel looked up, she saw Veronica standing in the doorway. "Why are you sorry? I'm the one who was mean to you. You didn't do nothin'."

"I did. I was mean to you too. And that was wrong. I didn't know about what had happened to you . . . being sick."

"And I didn't tell you, so that's my fault."

"But I could have tried to be nicer."

"We both could have," Veronica said softly.

Rachel put out her hand. "Think maybe we could start over?"

Wiping her eyes and allowing a smile to peek through, Veronica nodded her head yes. "Yeah . . . I think we can."

Rachel knew if there was ever a time to share her idea with her cousin, it was now.

"I've got an idea."

Obviously curious, Veronica gave Rachel her absolute full attention. "What kind of idea?"

"A beauty pageant . . . and I'll be in it, if you and your friends'll jump Double Dutch."

Veronica hesitated. "But I don't know how to . . ."

"That's not a problem. Marguerita said she knows how to jump, and between the two of us, we can show you and the rest of your friends how. Plus, I ain't never been in a beauty contest before, but I'd be willing to try."

Veronica pulled Rachel close, looked her squarely in the eye, and offered a confession. "I ain't never been in one either."

The two cousins laughed and saw that maybe they weren't so different after all.

Rachel was starting to understand what Coach Hughes meant when she encouraged her to learn new things. For it was in Chicago, while spending the summer with her cousin that an important lesson had almost been missed. It was like the time one Christmas morning two years ago when her parents had wrapped a box that contained a smaller box that contained another small box, then another. When Rachel finally opened the last tiny box, there inside was the beautiful opal ring she had been admiring in the window of a downtown jewelry store.

And again there was a lesson learned. Sometimes we must go past what we can see with our eyes in order to find the things in life that are truly special. Rachel was starting to look past the things Veronica had said and done and was seeking to find the jewel inside of her. She was pleased when she saw that Veronica was willing to learn. "I'll try," she said. "I'll try to learn how to jump Double Dutch."

Thinking about how little she knew about beauty contests, Rachel committed to trying to learn something new as well. "And I'm gonna be in a beauty pageant," she offered.

Veronica came closer. "So what do ya want to do first?"

"I think we need to find your friends," Rachel suggested. "Without them, we can't jump, and what kind of pageant could we have with only you and me?"

Rachel was surprised by Veronica's next comment. "I think the place to start is telling Marguerita I'm sorry for not being friendly to her. Even when I wasn't nice, she kept coming back. She really is a good friend, and I hope she'll be part of the pageant and wanna jump with us too."

Rachel smiled, knowing Marguerita wouldn't have any objections. As soon as she'd heard her mention jumping Double Dutch, her eyes sparkled with excitement. "How can we get in touch with your other friends? You know, the ones who didn't come to the luncheon."

"I think maybe if I go to each one of them and ask, there's a better chance they'll say yes."

"It's worth a try," Rachel said, supporting Veronica's choice to go to each one personally.

"After Marguerita, I think the next one should be Alyssa. I've known her the longest. Besides, if she says yes, I think Shonda will say yes too," Veronica said.

Rachel had a suggestion of her own. "Maybe we should ask Marguerita to come along with us."

Veronica smiled at Rachel's idea. "You're right. I think it'll be good if Marguerita comes too."

Now Rachel was the one with excitement in her eyes. Together they had a plan, and there was no time like the present to put it into action. "Then let's go," she said cheerfully. "Let's get Marguerita and then find Alyssa."

Marguerita was surprised when she opened her door to find Rachel and Veronica standing there. Veronica wasted no time offering her apology. "I'm sorry, Marguerita," she said. "I hope you still wanna be friends."

Marguerita wore a great big grin. "Sure I do."

"Me too," Veronica told her. "Wanna have a beauty pageant and jump some Double Dutch?"

"Definitely!" Marguerita shouted. "Who else ya got?"

"We're gonna ask Alyssa, and then Shonda. Alyssa only lives two blocks away, so we're going there now."

"Wanna come?" Rachel chimed in.

"Yeah, I'll come!"

One by one Veronica began mending the fences she had broken with her friends. She was surprised to find that none of them were so mad at her that they weren't willing to listen to what she had to say. Each one accepted her apology, and Veronica promised never to act like that again.

Rachel studied the array of friends Veronica had gathered and thought how much they reminded her of a bright bouquet of flowers. *Perhaps even a rainbow of people*, she thought.

Veronica's promise had brought everyone together again, and the result was a colorful picture of friendship. In the weeks to come, they could look ahead with great anticipation to their pageant and jumping Double Dutch. The one thing left to do now was for them to figure out how to put it all together.

Chapter Thirteen

Puttin' It All Together

WHEN Veronica's mom heard the girls' idea, she was quick to offer her help. She even told them about a lady in the neighborhood who she thought could get them started. Mrs. Agnes Miller was well known throughout the community mainly because she had been the Youth Director of Recreation for more than twenty years. So if there was an individual who knew the ins and outs of putting on any kind of community program or event, she was the person to see.

After having jumped in two Double Dutch competitions, Rachel needed no convincing about the necessity of seeing Mrs. Miller. She was fully aware of the importance of practicing and being well organized. She couldn't help but laugh when she thought about how she and the other girls had complained all those times when Coach Hughes made them exercise and run and jump until they felt like they had no energy left. However, looking back, now she could easily see the benefits they received from all that practicing. Whether she was studying for a test or working on her endurance for a jumping event, Rachel understood there was great value in preparing and getting things done.

Unfortunately, in spite of all their good intentions, everything was still up in the air concerning when and where the events would happen. Acknowledging they had no time to waste, the girls knew it was crucial for them to pay Mrs. Miller a visit. And Rachel was certain if they could get Mrs. Miller on board, as well as some of the adults to help, their plan would be successful.

"My parents'll help," Veronica offered. "I just have to ask them."

"But what would they do?" Marguerita inquired.

Shonda was quick to jump in with an answer to Marguerita's question. "It doesn't matter. There's so much to do that whatever they do will be great. I'm gonna ask my mom to help too. Maybe she'll help us with the pageant."

Alyssa, who didn't want to be left out, volunteered

her mother's services too. "Well, my mom knows how to sew. She can make those things for us."

None of the girls seemed to know what *things* Alyssa was referring to. "I think I know what she means," declared Shonda. Pretending she was wearing a sash, she began walking up and down the sidewalk. And everyone laughed when she added her own version of a beauty queen's wave.

"But what about the jumping part? I don't know how to jump Double Dutch!" Veronica reminded everyone.

"That's easy," Rachel assured her. "We're going to teach you how, and you can show me what I'm supposed to do in a beauty pageant."

Veronica looked stunned. "But I thought you said pageants were stupid!"

"You mean like you said Double Dutch was stupid?"

Veronica spoke softly. "I didn't mean it, ya know."

Rachel gently touched her cousin on the shoulder. "Me neither."

"Well, I can jump! And I can jump good!" shouted Marguerita. "We'll all help each other. The only thing we have to do now is get started."

Rachel was glad she'd packed her ropes and brought them to Chicago just in case an opportunity to jump Double Dutch came along. And she was more than excited that it appeared she would soon get her chance.

"Who'd wanna come and see us jump rope and

model in a beauty pageant?" asked Alyssa.

"Everybody!" Shonda bragged confidently. "I bet everybody'll come!"

"Like who?" Alyssa challenged.

Shonda was full of confidence. "The whole neighborhood's gonna come. You'll see!"

"Then we do need to go and see Mrs. Miller," Marguerita urged. "She only lives a coupla houses down the street from here. And I heard she used to do fashion shows and all kinds of stuff like that anyway when she worked for the rec center."

"You're right," Rachel agreed. "From what my Aunt Marion told us, she sounds like just the person we need to help us put this all together."

Veronica suddenly had a peculiar expression on her face.

Noticing the change, Rachel tried to find out what was wrong. "Why are you looking like that?" she asked.

"I think Mrs. Miller's kinda old."

"That can only mean one thing," Rachel responded.

"What's that?" Veronica asked.

"She knows a whole lot more about doin' this kinda stuff than we do," Shonda said. "So I say we ask her, and we do it right away."

"Me too!" said Alyssa.

"And me!" declared Marguerita.

Rachel looked at Veronica. "Well?"

Everyone could see Veronica was still a little reluctant, but she decided it was better to go along with the group. "Yeah," she said. "Let's ask Mrs. Miller to help us."

So the girls headed toward the other end of Euclid Street to see Mrs. Miller, hoping all the while she would consent to assist them in putting into action the plans for their summer event. Within minutes, the girls found themselves standing in front of house number 218. They waited there wondering what they should say and who was going to be brave enough to do the asking. They hadn't even decided who was going to knock at Mrs. Miller's door.

Marguerita was getting impatient. "But if we don't ask her, we'll never know if she woulda helped us."

"Then, you knock," Shonda encouraged. "I mean . . . since you said you knew her and everything."

"I didn't say I knew her. I said that I . . . ."

Before Marguerita had the chance to finish her sentence, the door to number 218 swung open and there standing in the doorway was a small gray-haired woman whose stare was very serious. "What's all this noise going on out here?" she demanded.

All of the girls, except Rachel stepped back a little. "We're sorry," she said. "Are you Mrs. Miller?"

"And if I am?" the woman asked.

"I . . . I mean, we need to talk to her."

Marguerita decided to take Rachel's lead and join in. "I heard she used to run the best recreation center in town. Are you *that* Mrs. Miller?"

Marguerita must have said something right because the elderly woman's face took on a warm glow and greeted the girls with a cheerful smile. "I did," she admitted.

Shonda got anxious and stepped up, aligning herself right next to Rachel. "Would you help us put together a beauty pageant and a Double Dutch jumping demonstration?"

"My, that sounds like a pretty big undertaking for five young ladies like yourselves. Besides, it's been a long time since I did any kind of show like that for the community."

Alyssa wasn't about to give up. "Please help us, Mrs. Miller!"

"Yeah," Rachel pleaded. "We'll be grateful for anything you can do."

The girls positioned themselves in a small semicircle and attempted to make their case all at once. "P-L-E-A-S-E!" they cried at the same time. They could tell Mrs. Miller was giving their request some consideration because she didn't immediately say no. "I'm not exactly sure what it is that you want, but all right . . . I'll help you."

"Yes!" Shonda shouted.

Rachel smiled and was grateful. "Thank you, Mrs. Miller!"

The girls were glad, and each one showed her gratitude by giving their newest friend a great big hug. Alyssa decided to ask Mrs. Miller the question that all of the girls probably had on their minds. "When will we start, and what should we do first?"

"Come back and see me in about two weeks." These were the words Mrs. Miller spoke to them as she began going back inside and slowly closing her door.

Rachel couldn't believe what she was hearing. "Two weeks? That'll only leave us five weeks left of summer."

Mrs. Miller's little smile disappeared, and her sweet tone changed back to the serious one that the girls had witnessed when she first emerged from her home. Hers was a demeanor that clearly spoke, "No nonsense." And after convincing her to help, Rachel didn't want to do anything to make her change her mind. "In those two weeks, be sure to use your time wisely," she advised. "Practice and plan out your ideas. You all have plenty of important things to do. Don't worry; I'll take care of what I can on my end."

"We will too," Marguerita said shyly. "Thank you, Mrs. Miller."

"So then we'll talk again in two weeks." Mrs. Miller stepped back inside and, without any further explanation, closed the door.

Shonda didn't look happy. "If we gotta wait two weeks to talk with her again, what are we supposed to be doing? I thought *she* was supposed to help us."

"Yeah, I don't get this," said Alyssa. "How are we gonna know what to do?"

"I'm wondering if she's gonna do anything at all," Veronica said. "Maybe she just wanted to get rid of us."

"But she did give her word, and that's like a promise," said Rachel. "Promises are important, and they're meant to be kept. I think she's gonna help just like she said she would. Our job right now is to make sure we can all jump Double Dutch. We can't have no kinda demonstration if we don't know how to do the thing we're supposed to be demonstrating in the first place. We need to go back to Veronica's," Rachel advised. "That's where we should start."

Veronica seemed a little confused. "Start what?"

"We're gonna *start* by teachin' you how to jump Double Dutch," Rachel assured her.

The minute they got to Veronica's, Rachel ran up the steps and into the house.

"Where's she going?" Shonda asked Veronica. Veronica shrugged her shoulders indicating she didn't know. But when Rachel quickly returned, everybody understood her sudden disappearance. In her hands she carried ropes. And they were the perfect size for jumping Double Dutch. "C'mon," she said, waving for the others to come near. "This is where we start puttin' it all together."

Shonda took one end of the ropes and Marguerita took the other. They began turning them inwardly at the same time and waited to see who would jump in first. "I'm ready to go!" Alyssa shouted as she did a quick side step inside the ropes.

"All you have to do right now is watch," Rachel told Veronica.

Each girl took a turn jumping in while they alternated turning duties to make sure everyone got a turn. Rachel could tell by the uneasy look on her cousin's face she was feeling intimidated. "You ready?" she asked Veronica.

"I don't know what to do," she said with her voice almost trembling.

Marguerita shouted while she continued turning. "Just jump in and make sure your feet keep moving! AND DON'T LOOK DOWN!"

Veronica looked at Rachel for reassurance. "That's the only way to learn. You just gotta do it."

So Veronica positioned herself close to the ropes. And when she thought the time was right, she made her first attempt to jump in. For the first six tries, she found herself entangled in the ropes. But on the seventh try, something special happened. Before she jumped in, she pictured the footsteps of each of the jumpers she'd watched. And somehow, though she couldn't explain it, Veronica found herself staying in step. Then from the top of her lungs, she proclaimed victory. "Look!" she yelled. "I got it! I got it!"

Rachel was overjoyed because for the first time since she arrived, she felt nothing but happiness. And she could see that Veronica was feeling it too. She watched her cousin jumping and beaming with joy all at the same time. Suddenly, Rachel understood how it was that her mother could feel good when she and Aunt Marion played as girls. *It's possible,* she thought, *to have good feelings from the good feelings of others. And that,* she told herself, *feels great.*

Chapter Fourteen

My Turn . . .

Uncle Walter was more than happy to relay the news that Mrs. Miller had been successful in getting the necessary permits the girls needed to hold their events. "Does that mean we can have the Double Dutch demonstration *and* the beauty pageant?" Veronica asked her father.

He looked at Veronica, Rachel, and his wife as though if he didn't hurry and share his good news he might simply burst from the joy of holding on to it. "Yes, it does. And you know what else? It's going to be a block party! The date is Saturday August 25th."

Rachel looked at Aunt Marion. "What's a block party?"

"I know what it is!" Veronica volunteered. "That's when a section of the street is closed off so all kinds of games and fun stuff can happen."

Rachel obviously had caught some of the excitement Uncle Walter had brought into the house. "You mean we get to jump that day . . . in front of everybody?"

"Everybody who wants to come," Uncle Walter assured her.

"And the pageant too?" Veronica asked.

"Yes," her father told her. "And they'll come to the pageant too."

Aunt Marion smiled because secretly she and some of the other mothers had been working on dresses for the pageant for weeks. In fact, except for a few finishing touches, they were almost done. "How's the jumping coming along?" she asked the girls.

Rachel decided to boast a bit. "It's coming along great!"

"I think I'm getting better," Veronica added. "But some days I'm not so sure."

"You're a lot better than you think," Rachel said, encouraging her.

"Thanks, but I still need a lot more practice."

Knowing how fast time was moving gave the girls incentive to practice each and every day. And by the time they had reached the end of the third week, Veronica was jumping Double Dutch as if she'd been doing it all her life. "It's my turn!" she yelled, running down the steps of her house and out the front door. "You're right!" Alyssa chuckled. "It is your turn to turn." She handed the ropes to Veronica while Marguerita and Shonda started laughing. It was easy to see that Veronica wasn't in a laughing mood. She threw the two pieces of rope to the ground, wiped her hands together, and began walking away as though signaling she was through. "It's a stupid game anyway."

Rachel was coming out the door when she met Veronica on her way back inside. "Where ya going? We need to practice. We can't do a demonstration if we're not ready."

"She's going in 'cause I told her she's supposed to turn," Alyssa called out.

Rachel couldn't understand the problem. "So what's the big deal?" she asked Veronica.

Veronica seemed less upset than just moments ago when she had thrown down the ropes. "I said it was my turn, and Alyssa laughed and put those ropes in my hands."

"I don't know how it's done in Chicago, but at my school we have a rule. If you don't turn, you don't jump. Now, did you turn today?"

Although reluctant to admit it, Veronica understood what everyone was trying to say. She peered back at the others. "No, I didn't. Guess I kinda messed up, huh?"

Rachel lightly tapped her arm to give her some reassurance. "We all do sometimes. It's not that serious."

Veronica turned all the way around, walked back down the steps, and picked up the ropes off the ground. "Who's jumping?"

"I am!" Alyssa hollered. Anxiously, she pointed at the other ends of the ropes. "Shonda, you take the other end."

"Oh, all right," Shonda said, picking up the other ends of the ropes from the ground. Veronica was ready with her end in her hands. Alyssa, Marguerita, and Rachel stood by anticipating the first leap inside to get the practice session started.

The two girls turned the ropes inwardly, eggbeater style, and began a swift cadence. The sound was a signal that it was time for the jumpers to come in. Rachel began rocking back and forth. There was a smile on her face that completely matched her entrance into the moving ropes. She'd only jumped for a few seconds when Marguerita jumped in behind her. "C'mon, Alyssa!" Marguerita screamed. "C'mon!"

She didn't have to say another word. Veronica and Shonda made sure there was enough room by giving some more rope as they turned. And pretty soon Alyssa was inside, jumping right along with Rachel and Marguerita.

"Give a high step! Give a high step!" Shonda shouted.

"Yeah," Veronica added. "It looks good. The only way it'll look better is when I get my turn."

Rachel agreed and jumped out of the ropes. She quickly slipped her hands over Veronica's and continued the turn without interruption. Marguerita did the same and came out too. She eased her hands over the portion of rope in front of Shonda so the turning wouldn't stop. The two girls studied the rhythm of the moving ropes and made sure they jumped in at the right time. Within seconds, Veronica and Shonda had joined Alyssa; the three of them moved their feet, turned, and jumped in perfect time. "You ain't tired?" Rachel shouted out to Alyssa.

"No," she said with excitement in her voice. "I could jump like this forever!"

"Me too!" Veronica shouted. "Me too!"

Chapter Fifteen

Gifts and Talents

It was Rachel's Aunt Marion who suggested each of the girls might share a talent just like the contestants did in real beauty pageants. "What do you mean?" Rachel asked. "What kind of talent? I don't think I have one."

"What can you do that you think is special?" her aunt questioned.

"I can dance!" Veronica offered. "That what you mean?"

"Yes, that's one example." She looked into the eyes

of the girls. "What about the rest of you? You all have special gifts and talents, you know. It's that part of what makes you, you. My grandma used to say, 'God gives everyone at least one special gift in this life. It's just a matter of finding out what it is.'"

"I can sing!" Shonda cried.

"I write songs sometimes," Alyssa offered. The girls all seemed amazed at hearing and learning of all the hidden talents that existed among them. They would have never guessed that Alyssa wrote songs or that Shonda liked to sing.

"That's wonderful!" Veronica's mother said.

"I can play the piano!" Marguerita offered proudly.

"What about you, Rachel?" her aunt inquired. "I'll bet if you think about it, you'll realize you've got something wonderful to share too."

Rachel thought real hard but seemed to be holding something back.

"C'mon, Rachel," Shonda urged. "We all told what we like to do."

"I like to write," Rachel answered softly. "I like to write poems about the things around me."

"Then share one of your poems!" Aunt Marion encouraged. "I'm already looking forward to hearing you recite one of your beautiful poems."

"Me too," Alyssa said, lending her new friend some support.

Rachel realized those standing around her had more confidence in her ability as a poet than she had in herself. "Okay," she relented. "I guess I'll share a poem." And from the second she said yes, she began wondering what she would write about. Her first thought was of the girls from the Double Dutch Club back home in New Jersey. But just as quickly as she considered them, she pictured herself writing something about the new friends she'd made this summer in Chicago. Rachel resolved that whatever she was going to write, she wanted it to be something meaningful.

The beginning of the summer had seemed to drag on slowly, but the next few weeks were some of the busiest Rachel had ever seen. And it was a time that was both exciting and wonderful to see the way people from all over the community were volunteering to help in any way they could. Somehow Mrs. Miller had even managed to get one of the civic groups around town to donate an outdoor stage where the girls could have their pageant and perform their Double Dutch demonstration.

If there were any extra minutes in the day, Rachel tried to use that time to come up with a topic for her poem. But as their special day was quickly approaching, she still hadn't a clue about anything she felt was worth putting on paper. And that made Rachel very uncomfortable. She began thinking that writing a poem was useless. *Maybe,* she told herself, *I should tell them I'm not ready and drop out of the pageant before it's too late.* However, the second the pep talk she had given Veronica about her jumping came to her remembrance, she convinced herself to hold out a little longer and say nothing about the possibility of giving up. That possibility, however, was starting to seem more and more real once Rachel found herself only six days away from the well-advertised "Euclid Street Block Party."

She was literally at a loss for words. Maybe Aunt Marion was wrong about everybody having a special gift or talent. If she'd ever had one, Rachel was starting to think she'd lost it. But just when the act of writing her poem seemed like it would never happen, she decided to ask God, who she knew was there, to help her. She remembered that He was with her even when she didn't realize it. Gazing out the window of her cousin's bedroom, which overlooked Euclid Street, Rachel spoke softly. "If ever there was a time when I could use Your help, Lord, it would be right now."

Chapter Sixteen

A Day to Remember

It was August 24th, the night before the big block party. And in spite of all the excitement surrounding what was probably going to be the most special day the people of Euclid Street had ever known, somehow Veronica had managed to fall asleep. From the peaceful look on her face, Rachel assumed her cousin was dreaming about tomorrow. Her quiet smile was a clear indication that in her dream she was already "jumping in" tomorrow.

Rachel, on the other hand, sat staring out the window wondering if she would ever finish her poem. She was satisfied with her title and had composed some words that she thought made a great beginning. However, every time she attempted to finish, she'd stop, stare at her paper, and convince herself to return to it later. "I'll tell them I couldn't do it," she said, climbing back into bed.

Rachel finally felt her eyelids getting heavy, so she closed her eyes and hoped to get a good night's rest. She had been asleep only for a little over an hour when a loud crash of thunder awakened her. She glanced over at Veronica and wondered how she was able to continue sleeping through so much noise. Maybe she was tired from all the practicing she'd done. Coach Hughes would often tell the team, "If you practice as much as you should, your reward at the least will be a well-deserved good night's sleep."

Rachel glanced again at Veronica and said, "She deserves it. Nobody's put in as much work as she has."

It wasn't long before that first crash of thunder became a full-fledged storm with bolts of lightning and heavy rain closely following. Those were the sounds Rachel remembered as she fell off to sleep for the rest of the night: the sound of the thunder, flashes of lightning, and pouring rain.

When Rachel and Veronica awakened the next morning, they opened their eyes to find two beautiful dresses hanging neatly in front of the closet door. One was a delicate mint green while the other was a soft shade of periwinkle blue. And each girl knew immediately which one was hers. Rachel's favorite color was blue, and Veronica's was green. They sprang themselves out of bed and hurried to get the dresses down.

"Thank you, Mom and Dad!" Veronica yelled downstairs to her parents. "Yeah, thank you both!" Rachel hollered.

"You're welcome, and I hope you like them!" Aunt Marion stood at the bottom of the stairs. "You two need to try and pull yourselves away from your dresses and come down for breakfast."

"We will!" Veronica answered.

The two girls looked at each other and smiled. Rachel held her dress gently. "It's beautiful," she said as she softly brushed her hand over the satiny material.

"Mine is too," said Veronica.

Thankfully, during the weeks that had passed, the friction existing between them since the start of summer had disappeared. And suddenly, all the differences they had mounted against each other that would keep them apart had gone away for good. Standing in front of the mirror, they held their dresses close, just below their necks, and smiled at each other with lots of approval. They hugged their dresses as though lovingly holding their very first dolls.

Placed on the floor were two identical pairs of lovely white patent leather shoes. The squeals of joy filling the room came to an abrupt end when clamorous sounds of the returning thunderstorm chased away their laughter. Rachel realized the storm had apparently only been resting from the night before. It had now returned and done so with such force that it couldn't be ignored.

Rachel and Veronica rushed over to the window, pressing their faces hard against it, staring down at a rain-soaked Euclid Street. It appeared their plans were ruined. Without uttering a word, they quietly laid their dresses across the bed and went downstairs to have breakfast. Rachel's Aunt Marion could see disappointment written all over their faces. She wanted to encourage them, but a quick peek out the kitchen window made choosing the right words extremely hard. She wanted to say something to lift their spirits but knew, if it continued to rain, whatever words she spoke would unfortunately be meaningless.

"Eat something," she told the girls. "It will take your mind off the weather. Maybe it will stop soon."

Rachel looked at Veronica, and Veronica looked at Rachel. It was as if their two separate thoughts miraculously became one. Nothing could take their minds off the weather right now—not even the delicious plates of bacon and eggs that had been set before them. Neither of them would touch even a morsel of food, and Aunt Marion knew that trying to get them to eat at this point was hopeless.

Uncle Walter figured this might be a good time for one of his stories. "I remember when I used to run track," he said. "We had a storm like this." He sat up straight and used his hands to help tell the story. "It was the biggest meet of our whole season! And it had been raining for days. And on one of those days it rained for ten straight hours. I didn't think it would ever stop."

Veronica was curious. "Did it?" she asked anxiously. It was obvious she wanted him to say yes.

"No," he said, losing some of the volume in his voice. "It took more than a week for the field where the track was located to dry out. And by the time we got our chance, we didn't run with the same vigor we would have had on that day."

Rachel could tell what was coming next.

"Did you win?" Veronica asked her father.

Uncle Walter's answer harbored a hint of sadness. "No, we didn't." When he saw Veronica drop her head, he knew that his story hadn't helped the situation at all and had probably made matters worse.

Rachel got up from her seat and went to the front door. She opened it and watched the falling rain totally obscure the very street which later that afternoon was supposed to be filled with music and the laughter of neighbors and friends. She ran upstairs, stood in front of the window, and mouthed the words, "Please God, stop the rain so we can have our day."

She walked over to the bed and reached under her pillow to retrieve the partially written poem from the night before. She stared at the words she had composed and waited for more to join them. Her paper remained blank, so again she went to the window. To her dismay, nothing had changed for the better. Crumbling the paper in her hand, she shoved it under her pillow, and laid herself across the bed. Rachel closed her eyes, wishing she could fall asleep and start the day all over again. "This time," she told herself, "when I wake up, I hope the sun will be shining everywhere."

Unfortunately, Rachel didn't get the chance to find out if her plan to sleep away the rain would have worked. The minute she rested her head against the pillow, she could hear Veronica calling from downstairs. "Rachel! Hurry up and c'mon. We've gotta lot to do!"

Rachel wanted to tell her cousin to forget the plans they'd made. It was very clear that the great event they'd told everyone about and made countless flyers for wasn't going to take place. However, another part of her wanted to show the kind of enthusiasm she heard in Veronica's voice. She almost acted as if there was no storm. Veronica intended to continue getting ready for the afternoon just as if she had been greeted by the sun that morning.

Rachel slowly got up and dragged herself downstairs. "Sit down," Veronica said cheerfully. "My mom's gonna do our hair, and you're gonna be first."

Rachel was amazed. *Do our hair for what?* she thought. *Don't they know it's raining outside?* Even while she was silently asking herself a million questions, Rachel sat down and allowed her aunt to create for her a hairstyle worthy of a beautiful young princess. When Aunt Marion was done, she handed Rachel a mirror and both she and Veronica knew that Rachel was pleased. "It's so pretty," she said, turning her head from side to side. "Thank you, Aunt Marion. I really like it."

"You're welcome, and it was my pleasure. Your mother and I used to make such pretty hairstyles when we were growing up."

Veronica was quick to help Rachel out of her seat. "Okay, Mom, now me! I want something nice and special too."

Rachel was happy to see that it was Veronica's own hair that she wanted her mother to style. The wig was gone.

Rachel watched intently as Aunt Marion created a second hairdo. Although it was quite different, it was equally befitting any young beautiful princess. This time, Rachel picked up the mirror and handed it to Veronica. However, before she could place it in her hand, something she saw reflected in the mirror grabbed her attention. Veronica lifted her head and smiled. The same exquisite ray of sunshine that had managed to sneak its way through the kitchen window had also streaked across the mirror Rachel held so proudly in her hand.

Immediately, the girls jumped up and ran to the front door. The storm had ended, and they knew everything was going to be all right. Aunt Marion put her arms around the girls' shoulders and stood with them right in the middle of that sunbeam and smiled. "I think we'd better call Uncle Walter and start setting up."

Rachel looked up and stared out at the bright blue sky above her and knew God had answered her prayer. The rain had stopped, and the sun was shining itself proudly all over Euclid Street. It was early enough and hot enough that the street was already beginning to dry. And everyone from vendors to onlookers had already begun to assemble themselves along both sides of the street.

With her lawn chair in hand, Mrs. Miller was one of the first to arrive. She scouted out what she considered "the perfect spot" right in front of the stage. The pageant was scheduled to be the first event of the afternoon, and Mrs. Miller was the girls' choice to announce it.

The girls met in Veronica's room and were busily getting themselves ready. They could hear the sound of musical instruments being played outside and ran to the window to see. Marguerita shouted as she pointed out the window. "That's Mr. Taylor, the dry cleaner, from up the street! I didn't know he played guitar."

Shonda pushed her way through the rest of the girls to get a better look. "And that's Officer Watkins playing the drums! People really do have all kinds of talents that we don't know about."

There were clowns who juggled as they walked through the middle of the street greeting everyone. There was also a special table where young children were getting their faces painted. And free balloons were given to anyone who wanted one, while the freshly cooked aroma of grilled hamburgers and hot dogs traveled up through Veronica's window.

"Ummm," Shonda said. "Soon as we're done, I'm getting something to eat." She turned to Rachel. "Got your poem?"

Rachel's silence caused everyone to look squarely in her direction. "I started it and had some trouble, but it's done."

"Can we hear it? I'll sing some of my song if you read the poem you wrote," Shonda offered.

"And I'll show you my dance," Veronica chimed in with what she considered a fair exchange.

Rachel could see the street below was filling up with people and was relieved there wasn't enough time to read. "I'd better not. The pageant is first, remember? I think we'd better get down there."

Knowing that their beauty pageant and Double Dutch demonstration were the two highlighted events for the afternoon, the girls finished getting themselves ready. Anyone who saw the way they helped one another would never have guessed they were preparing for a competition. They were careful to make sure every strand of hair was in place and that their beautiful dresses of colorful fabric looked "just so."

As they lined themselves up in front of the mirror, Rachel saw something she considered astounding. With each girl wearing the dress of her favorite color and a matching flower in her hair, there was no doubt that everyone looked pretty. But as they stood side by side, together they took on the elegance of a beautiful floral bouquet.

"It's time for the pageant to begin!" Aunt Marion yelled, summoning the girls to come downstairs. They left the room in a cloud of giggles and screams of joy. Not one of them knew the first thing about how to hold a beauty pageant, so they were very glad Mrs. Miller had consented to act as their announcer. And though admittedly nervous, having her there made them feel a little more at ease.

By the time they got outside, Mrs. Miller had left her chair and stood confidently onstage, waving her hand and encouraging the girls to join her. Walking through the huge crowd of people wasn't easy, but when everyone started applauding their entrance, they found themselves feeling very special. Therefore, ascending the stage wasn't nearly as hard as they'd thought it would be.

Mrs. Miller told all of the girls to stand to the far right of the stage—out of view—while she quickly and carefully made sure the note cards in her hands were arranged correctly. She nodded her head for the music to begin and signaled for Marguerita to walk out to the front of the stage. "First, we have Miss Marguerita Lopez, wearing a beautiful pink dress with lovely rose accents." As Mrs. Miller continued her description, Marguerita walked cautiously across the stage and waved to an enormous crowd of onlookers.

"Thank you, Marguerita," Mrs. Miller said as Marguerita returned to the right corner of the stage to make way for the next contestant in the pageant.

Mrs. Miller continued announcing each girl and gave a wonderful description of the pretty dresses they wore until all had a turn to grace the stage. Once the introductions and descriptions were finished, it was time for the talent portion of the program to begin. There were singing and dancing performances, and Marguerita played an original song on her keyboard. And by the sound of the applause coming from the audience, they really liked what they saw and heard.

Rachel was the last of the girls scheduled to share her talent. Standing in front of the microphone nervously holding the piece of paper that held the contents of her poem, she refrained from looking at the audience. "Go ahead, child," Mrs. Miller could be heard saying in the background. "You may begin."

Rachel wanted to speak but felt like someone had poured sand down her throat. She stared intently at the words on the page, but speaking them seemed impossible. "C'mon, Rachel," she heard someone call out from the crowd. The voice was both encouraging and familiar. She lifted her head and scanned the many faces in front of her. Suddenly her eyes met with two smiling faces that she knew all too well. Rachel lifted her hand and waved excitedly to her proud parents who had come from New Jersey to attend the Euclid Street Block Party. They had come to see their daughter jump Double Dutch and participate in her first beauty pageant.

Mr. Carter pointed and signaled for Rachel to look upward and to her left. Her eyes sparkled and widened as she found herself witnessing the second rainbow of her life. Rachel again recalled the words her father told her during the storm. "God is always with you. It is one of His promises, so there is no need to be afraid." A huge smile broke out across Rachel's face. She observed the faces of her audience, cleared her throat with a cough, and spoke softly. "The title of my poem is 'A Promise and a Rainbow.'"

Promises so often spoken,
We hope and pray,
They won't be broken.
But many tend to come apart,
And when they do,
It pains the heart.
But there is One who keeps His Word,
His strength is great,
Have you not heard?
He gives us rainbows,
And sets them high,
Reminders we should always try
To learn new things; to make new friends,
And when we're wrong,
To make amends.
I've learned that life can be brand-new.
If I believe,
His promises are true!
A promise from God can even grow,
Into the most beautiful, colorful, and grandest rainbow!

The immediate and thunderous applause let Rachel know her audience of listeners enjoyed her poem. Mrs. Miller then called for all the girls to come forth to the front of the stage. She helped them form a straight line, and they could barely stand still as they waited for the announcement that would declare the winner of the pageant.

To the girls' surprise, Rachel's Aunt Marion and Uncle Walter joined them onstage and presented each girl with a lovely silver crown and a trophy. Veronica closed her eyes as her parents gently placed the crown upon her head. When they finished, she reached up and touched it to make sure she wasn't dreaming. "You are all pageant winners!" Mrs. Miller announced joyfully. "And we congratulate each of you."

Upon hearing the results, each of the girls smiled and greeted everyone with her very own rendition of a traditional pageant waving of her hand. Rachel was relieved because she knew the hardest part for her was over. She was more than ready for what she considered the biggest event of the day—the Double Dutch demonstration.

Quickly exiting the stage, the girls headed straight for Veronica's room to get themselves ready. Forgetting about the pretty clothes and the dressy shoes they were wearing, they charged up the stairs and into the room. Someone had placed five T-shirts of different colors on the bed, and right away, they began claiming them. Alyssa was the first to get hers. She grabbed the bright red one and charged over to the mirror to see how it looked. "I got mine," she cheered.

"Me too!" Marguerita said excitedly. "Mine is the yellow one."

"I'll take the green!" Veronica shouted. "And Rachel wants the blue one . . . right, Rachel?"

"That's right," Rachel said, holding out her hand.

"Well, there's only one left. And that's got to be mine," Shonda told them. "And you're all lucky it's orange 'cause that just happens to be my favorite color."

Once the colors were chosen, no time was wasted in putting on the brightly colored tees, crisp denim jeans, and white sneakers.

"We're ready," said Alyssa.

"And we look good!" Marguerita bragged.

"It's a rainbow," Rachel uttered quietly, while her eyes glistened in amazement.

Alyssa stepped out in front and led the charge. "C'mon, let's go jump Double Dutch!"

One by one, the girls filed out of the door, down the stairs, and back outside to the waiting crowd. When they took to the stage, there waiting to introduce them for the second big event of the afternoon was Mrs. Miller. To their surprise, she too was wearing a brightly colored T-shirt as well. Hers was a rich, royal purple. After making sure the girls were ready, she signaled for the music to start so the jumping could begin.

Marguerita and Shonda turned first, while Rachel, Veronica, and Alyssa were set to jump in. Veronica was a little nervous because she knew it was time to start their routine. Just as they had practiced, she let Rachel jump in first, while she made sure to count every step. She waited carefully, rocking back and forth the way Rachel had taught her. On the count of five, she leaped inside the ropes and mimicked every move her cousin made. Each time Rachel's left foot touched the stage, so did Veronica's. If Rachel lifted her hands, Veronica lifted hers too.

Just as Rachel told her, she was careful not to look down as she jumped. As long as she followed her cousin's lead, she knew everything was all right. Then Rachel and Veronica carefully eased themselves out of the ropes; each took an end from Shonda and Marguerita, while Alyssa continued jumping.

The minute Marguerita and Shonda vaulted themselves in, Alyssa leaped out and allowed the two of them to dazzle the crowd with their speed. Rachel cheered them on from her end, and Veronica did the same. "You can do it! You can do it!" they shouted.

As soon as Alyssa put up her hand signaling that a minute had passed, she moved next to Rachel and took her end of the ropes. Without any hesitation at all, Rachel jumped in and took the third spot inside the turning ropes. The three girls created spins, leaps, and jumped on one foot, alternating from one to the other. Throughout the performance, they never missed a single step. Just as the music was ending, one at a time they each came out of the ropes and bowed gracefully to the onlooking crowd of people. Veronica and Alyssa placed the end of the ropes on the stage and each took her place in line and bowed with the rest of the girls.

Rachel felt happy about the way her summer was ending. She was proud of what she and Veronica, along with the other girls, had been able to accomplish together. She looked out at the cheering crowd and smiled, knowing they had played an important part in doing something that made so many people feel good. Coach Hughes had been right about meeting new people and trying new things. It really was fun—and that made this a summer Rachel would always remember.

She couldn't wait to tell all her friends back home in New Jersey that not only had she been able to jump Double Dutch, she was in a beauty pageant too. She thought how interesting it was that something she hadn't wanted to do had turned out to be something so wonderful.

Rachel stood onstage and looked from left to right at Veronica, Marguerita, Shonda, and Alyssa. She waved to her parents and thanked God for the rainbows. She realized now that besides the rainbows He places in the sky, God sometimes places rainbows before us. For we see them in the smiles and the happiness of those standing right in front of us.

ISBN: 978-0-8024-2251-4

The girls of the Double Dutch Club have an opportunity of a lifetime: they've earned the right to compete in the state competition! What begins as a desire in their hearts to win a coveted trophy becomes the foundation for relationships that last a lifetime.

by Mabel E. Singletary
Find it now at your favorite local or online bookstore.

ISBN: 978-0-8024-2252-1

In the sequel to *Just Jump*, the girls from Grover Elementary return for the new school year only to learn that Ming, their wise leader, has returned to China with her family. They'll have to find someone else to jump Double Dutch with them in time for the December Jump Off. Meanwhile, tough Tanya keeps bumping heads with a new student, Brittany, and is surprised to find the new girl can stand her ground in a fight. Join the adventure in book two of *The Double Dutch Club Series*.

by Mabel Singletary

Available soon at your favorite local or online bookstore.

www.LiftEveryVoiceBooks.com

THE PAYTON SKKY SERIES

The Payton Skky series tells of the spiritual struggles and temptations of Christian high school student Payton Skky. Facing issues such as sexuality, alcohol and drugs, unsaved friends, depression, and the trials of dating puts Payton's faith to the test.

Staying Pure
978-0-8024-4236-9

Sober Faith
978-0-8024-4237-6

Saved Race
978-0-8024-4238-3

Sweetest Gift
978-0-8024-4239-0

Surrendered Heart
978-0-8024-4240-6

by Stephanie Perry Moore
Find it now at your favorite local or online bookstore.

www.LiftEveryVoiceBooks.com

The Negro National Anthem

Lift every voice and sing
Till earth and heaven ring,
Ring with the harmonies of Liberty;
Let our rejoicing rise
High as the listening skies,
Let it resound loud as the rolling sea.
Sing a song full of the faith that the dark past has taught us,
Sing a song full of the hope that the present has brought us,
Facing the rising sun of our new day begun
Let us march on till victory is won.

So begins the Black National Anthem, written by James Weldon Johnson in 1900. Lift Every Voice is the name of the joint imprint of The Institute for Black Family Development and Moody Publishers.

Our vision is to advance the cause of Christ through publishing African-American Christians who educate, edify, and disciple Christians in the church community through quality books written for African-Americans.

Since 1988, The Institute for Black Family Development, a 501(c)(3) non-profit Christian organization, has been providing training and technical assistance for churches and Christian organizations. The Institute for Black Family Development's goal is to become a premier trainer in leadership development, management, and strategic planning for pastors, ministers, volunteers, executives, and key staff members of churches and Christian organizations. To learn more about The Institute for Black Family Development, write us at:

The Institute for Black Family Development
15151 Faust
Detroit, Michigan 48223

We hope you enjoy this book from Moody Publishers. Our goal is to provide high-quality, thought-provoking books and products that connect truth to your real needs and challenges. For more information on other books and products written and produced from a biblical perspective, go to www. moodypublishers.com or write to:

Moody Publishers/LEV
820 N. LaSalle Blvd.
Chicago, Illinois 60610
www.moodypublishers.com